SEDIGITUS SWIFT

The Misadventures of Thonir

Archelaus

Washington, DC

Published by *Archelaus*

archelaus-cards.com

This is a work of fiction. All of the characters and events portrayed in it are products of the author's imagination, as is Sedigitus Swift himself.

Cover art by Glen Evans

ISBN 978-1-961852-09-9 (paperback)
ISBN 978-1-961852-08-2 (ebook)

The Misadventures of Thonir

Tales from Ondiran, Book Four

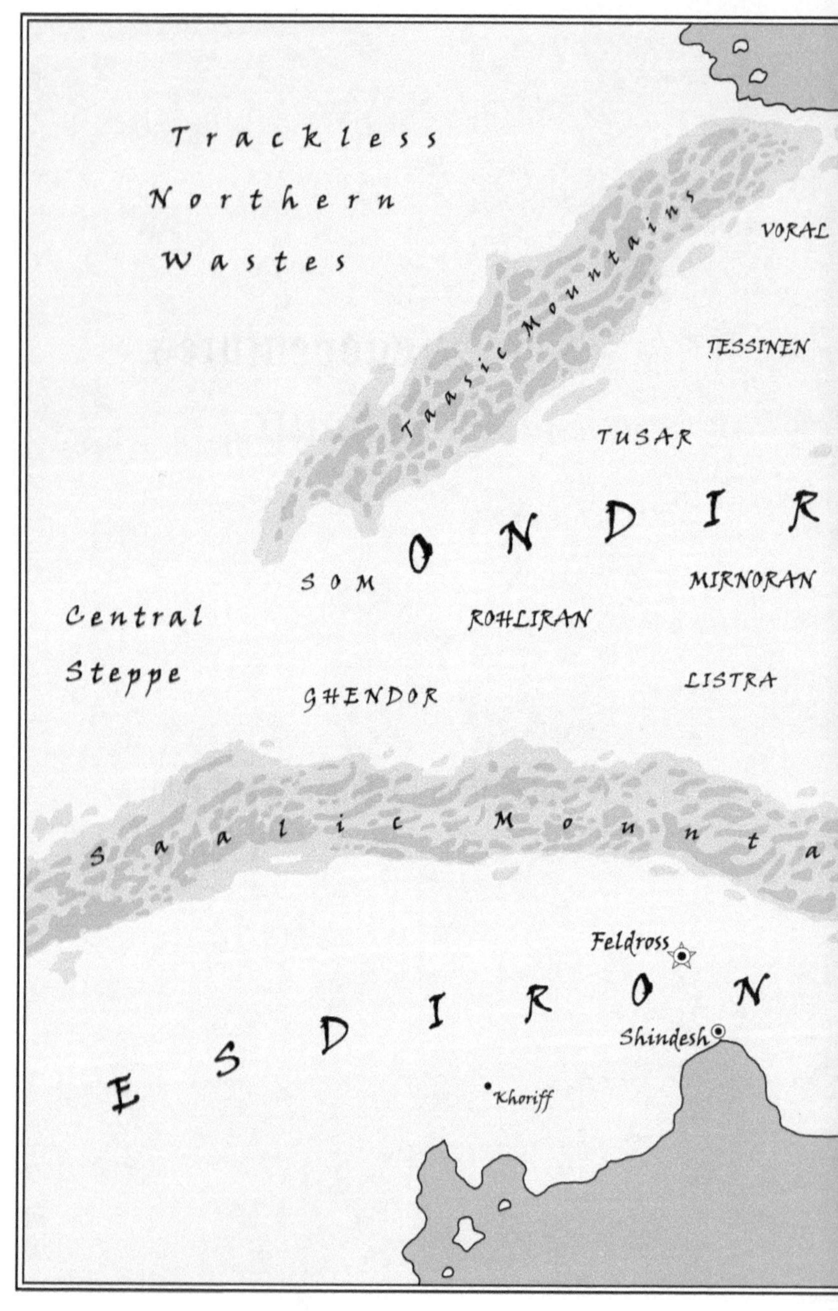

Trackless Northern Wastes
Taasic Mountains
VORAL
TESSINEN
TUSAR
ONDIR
SOM
MIRNORAN
Central Steppe
ROHLIRAN
LISTRA
GHENDOR
Saalic Mounta
Feldross
ESDIRON
Shindesh
Khoriff

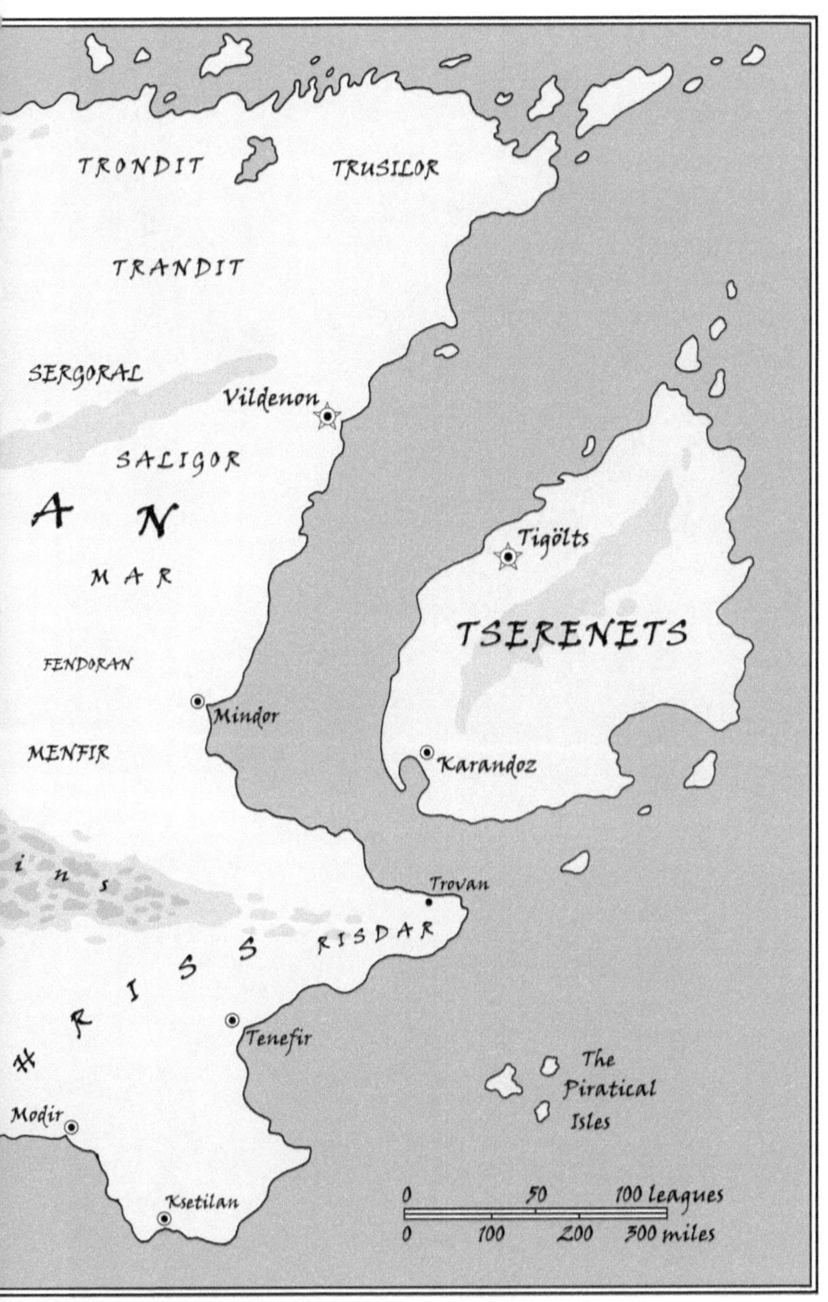

TRONDIT
TRUSILOR
TRANDIT
SERGORAL
Vildenon
SALIGOR
A N
M A R
Tigölts
TSERENETS
FENDORAN
Mindor
MENFIR
Karandoz
i n s
Trovan
R I S S   RISDAR
R I
Tenefir
The
Piratical
Isles
Modir
Ksetilan
0   50   100 leagues
0   100   200   300 miles

1

Condemned to death for the heinous crimes of conspiracy and high treason, the foreign wizard Chodros was disemboweled on the Bloodstone by the city headsman Master Tor. To the last the scoundrel refused to confess or repent.

— *Chronicle of the Ducal City of Mindor*

The distinctive toll of the prison bell quickly drew a crowd, eager to follow the tumbrel that must soon emerge from the prison gate and carry the condemned man to his death. Six weeks had passed since the shocking exposure of a plot to assassinate his grace, Lord Tothril, Eighth Duke of Mindor in the Empire of Ondiran. Seven accused conspirators had already been executed, and the city was alive with rumors that today was finally the day for the wizard Chodros, the alleged ringleader, to join them. The previous executions, which included two of the wizard's servants, had been suitably gruesome, so the populace had understandably high expectations for this one—as did the vendors of spicy sausage, roasted chestnuts, and warm beer, who hastened to wheel their carts out through Badger's Gate to the large field holding the execution platform, known locally as the Bloodstone.

With their throngs of excited, distracted spectators, public executions also present a prime opportunity for pickpockets and cutpurses. The death knell therefore served as an urgent summons for the denizens of Dob the Fence's dockside warehouse—including their latest recruit, Thonir, a scruffy sixteen-year-old, whose short black hair looked as though he had cut it with a penknife, as in fact he had. Unlike many of his companions, however, Thonir detested executions, along with the exemplary floggings, brandings, and maimings to which those convicted of lesser crimes were routinely subjected on the Bloodstone. Small for his age, he had been much bullied by larger boys as a youngster, and this mistreatment—while kindling an enduring spark of rage deep inside him—had also instilled an abhorrence of cruelty and all who perpetrated it.

To be sure, Thonir had a personal reason to frown on this particular execution, for up until the day of Chodros's arrest six weeks earlier he had been the wizard's apprentice.

Thonir had been lucky to avoid arrest himself. Sent to a nearby alchemist's shop to procure ingredients for one of Chodros's potions, he had returned to find members of the city watch leading the wizard's servants away in chains, while even more dramatic events played out within the wizard's house itself. Presently, the duke's personal sorcerer emerged, looking uncharacteristically disheveled, followed by eight watchmen, two of whom were dragging an unconscious Chodros.

His pulse racing, Thonir hastened to slip away before anyone noticed him. Finding temporary sanctuary in an Asardian temple, he struggled to compose his thoughts while pretending to pray. He was at a loss to see how he would now complete his magical training. Chodros was the only wizard in the ducal city, perhaps in the entire duchy (sorcery being the prevailing system of magic there), but even if he were not, who would risk taking on an apprentice whose previous master had been arrested? Wizardry was more prevalent in the Duchy of Hriss, some seventy leagues to the south, but that was a daunting journey for a boy who had never traveled more than a few miles beyond the city walls. He could not return home to his parents, either. Both had died four years earlier, shortly after he began his apprenticeship, during one of the frequent epidemics to sweep the city. Nor could he turn to friends, for at this point he had no one close. Working with Chodros had been isolating, and he had soon grown apart from his pre-apprenticeship playmates. He was, he concluded, very much alone and would have to rely upon his own resources.

Admittedly, these appeared to consist of little more than a few spells, plus the handful of small coins he had received in change at the alchemist's shop. Having no immediate use for the potion ingredients he had bought, he went back in the hope of returning them. The alchemist, however, had caught wind of Chodros's arrest in the meantime and took unabashed advantage of the boy's vulnerable position by refusing to buy back the ingredients for more than a quarter of their earlier purchase price. Thonir knew a useful charm spell and cast it covertly in the hope of obtaining a better deal, but the experienced old man not only resisted the attempt to influence him but retaliated, reducing his offer by half. Disgusted, the boy took the money and left, before the alchemist could cut the figure further.

Risky though he knew it would be, Thonir was determined to salvage anything he could from Chodros's house. He had spent years painstakingly copying out whatever Chodros had been willing to teach him, and while he had committed much of it to memory, no magician can remember everything—or, frankly, more than a small fraction of everything. Recovering his notes was therefore a high priority. As the sun set in the early evening, he stole back through the gradually emptying streets to the wizard's townhouse. Over four hundred years old (if the date over the door was to be believed), it was a ramshackle structure, as Chodros had little patience for such mundane matters as routine maintenance. An ominously large member of the city watch stood guard at the door.

"The duke's sorcerer has sent me to retrieve more of the wizard's papers," Thonir announced, as confidently as he could. A charm spell, he knew, stood a better chance of success if accompanied by a plausible story. "As you can see, he's given me the wizard's key." He produced his own. *Now stand aside and let me pass!* To his relief, the watchman stepped away from the door with no more than an idle remark about the weather.

Thonir was not surprised to find the contents of the house turned upside down. He started in his own room. Vexingly, his lesson notes were gone. Fortunately, the watchmen had not found his secret place beneath the floorboards. Chodros had not been a generous teacher: he was secretive by nature, and apprenticing under him had taught Thonir to be devious. The boy rescued various scraps of parchments on which he had surreptitiously copied spells the master had not chosen to share. He also retrieved a pilfered piece of enchanted chalk (used for drawing protective circles), his meager savings from four years of paltry pocket money, and the penknife his father had given him, along with a small whetstone he had bought to keep it sharp. He then gathered his spare set of clothes, which the watchmen had strewn about the floor, and rolled them up in the woolen blanket from his bed.

Moving on to Chodros's study, he found a scene of even greater disorder. All of the wizard's books and papers were gone, but he was pleased to find an empty leather tube, in which he could carry his rolled-up parchments. Even better, the watchmen had not recognized Chodros's enchanted self-inking quill for what it was. Unfortunately, the duke's sorcerer had found and cleaned out the wizard's two hiding places, only one of which Thonir had known about himself.

The watchmen had helped themselves to most of the food in the kitchen and pantry, notwithstanding its negligible evidentiary value. Thonir was nonetheless able to scrounge half a loaf of day-old bread and a little cheese. He also took a spoon, a knife, and a wooden drinking cup, as well as a flint and steel from next to the fireplace. He knew how to produce fire by magic, but it never hurt to have a backup method. Finally, he found a sack in which to stash his various treasures. If he was to survive life on the streets, he would need them.

Thonir caught up with the tumbrel shortly after it reached Badger's Gate. Chodros had been fitted with an engraved steel and brass "magician's collar," a device enchanted to drain away the wearer's magical power, rendering him unable to cast spells. He nevertheless stood defiantly erect, while the executioner heated a large pair of iron tongs in a cauldron of flaming pitch prepared there in advance by his assistant. "Nip him!" shouted someone in the crowd. "Nip the Esdiric bastard!" (The Ondir did not much care for the Esdir, and the ornery wizard had done little over the years to dissuade his neighbors from their prejudice.) The executioner first lifted the tongs high in the air, so the crowd could see they were glowing red, then brought them together, first upon his victim's left bicep, then upon his right, as dictated by the sentence of the court. Each time there was a brisk sizzle, and the scent of burning flesh wafted over the crowd. Chodros, who was a tough old bird, managed not to scream, but he could not help groaning loudly through clenched teeth. The crowd cheered and whistled, as though they were attending a sporting event.

Thonir swore softly. He had little affection for Chodros, who had been a hard master, but he had no wish to see the man suffer. The entire barbaric spectacle—which would shortly get much worse—repelled him. He knew a spell that would anesthetize Chodros against the worst of the pain (ironically, one of those Chodros had declined to teach him), but the execution of the wizard's housekeeper two weeks earlier had taught him to wait. Balancing the strength of the spell and its duration required a high degree of fine control and judgment. By expending every last bit of his magical power (called *silendras* in the mystical language of wizardry —or *korethi* in the mystical language of sorcery), he had been able to spare the housekeeper the agony of the tongs, only to see the spell wear off before the ordeal of the actual execution was over.

Accordingly, he now followed the tumbrel the rest of the way to the Bloodstone, where he deferred his spell until the last possible moment. The wizard was given a chance to confess his crimes and express contrition, but he declined to do either, instead protesting his innocence and denouncing the proceedings that had convicted him. He thereby not only angered the crowd but encouraged the executioner to show no mercy when he sliced open Chodros's abdomen and began slowly to extract his intestines.

Thonir put everything he had into his anesthetizing spell, enabling Chodros to display an astonishing degree of sangfroid as his horrific ordeal went forward. The boy then turned his back on the Bloodstone, having no desire to watch. He was, in any case, supposed to be there to steal.

While Thonir might have been friendless and alone following Chodros's arrest, unfortunately that did not mean that no one in the city knew him. He had therefore quickly done what he could to alter his appearance. Exchanging the respectable garb of an apprentice for some worn-out rags helped, as well as bringing in a few more small coins (though he kept his spare set of clothes in the wistful hope of someday wearing them again). He cut his shoulder-length hair and rubbed a little dirt into it. He also smeared some dirt on his face. On a superficial level, at least, the transformation from Thonir, wizard's apprentice, to Thon, street urchin, was complete. Adjusting mentally to the setback in his fortunes would take longer.

He had enough money to keep himself fed for the first few days, but sleeping rough proved unpleasant, for the spring weather still grew cold at night. Even worse was avoiding conflict with the more aggressive elements of the city's criminal underclass. Indeed, his initial encounter with members of Dob's juvenile band was fraught with danger, and he had avoided coming to harm only by the use of magic. When word of the incident got back to Dob, however, the kidsman readily saw the value of obtaining a homeless boy magician for his stable of delinquents and immediately set out to recruit him in person.

Dob was an unprepossessing man in his mid-fifties, with watery blue eyes, a bad limp, and a scraggly brown beard streaked with gray, but there was little he did not know about thievery or the ins and outs of the Mindoric demimonde. He dressed unobtrusively and carried a lead-cored walking stick with which he could, when he thought it necessary, deliver quite a wallop. On this occasion, understanding the mentality of the typical sixteen-year-old boy, he brought with him a comely sixteen-year-old girl, the raven-haired Ora, who was perhaps inevitably known by the nickname "Oraminta" (the Ondiric word for a type of delectable fruit-filled pastry).

To be sure, Dob would have had no great difficulty persuading Thonir to join him, even without the help of the alluring Oraminta. Four days and five nights on the street had left the boy singularly receptive to the promise of a roof over his head, food in his belly, and protection from urban predators. He was not so naive as to imagine that Dob was a trustworthy character (anymore than that Oraminta would take a genuine interest in him), but he calculated that so long as he made himself useful, Dob would have cause to regard him as an asset and treat him accordingly.

❧

Having no training as a pickpocket initially, Thonir had adopted the guise of a beggar child and relied upon charm spells to induce people to surrender coins to him. Knowing he would have no *silendras* to spare on charms when the day of Chodros's execution came, the boy had held back some of his takings on previous good days, so as to have a respectable sum to surrender to Dob afterward. He used magic to avoid being detected in doing so, because the kidsman was keenly aware that his charges were tempted to "skim" for their own profit, and he punished it harshly.

As the execution began, Thonir went through the motions of begging all the same, pleading for alms from the bloodthirsty crowd, but without the help of charms he was having a thin time of it. He had already had his ears boxed twice, when an indignant cooper grabbed him firmly by the arm and began to belabor him with a hoop driver, the short iron-shod wooden tool used to force hoops down into position on barrels.

"You want my hard-earned brass? Take that, you slothful boy!" the cooper shouted. "And that!"

Unlike the rest of the gang, whom Dob paired off to pick pockets (the "bumper" to distract the mark and the "lifter" to steal the purse), Thonir operated alone, which

9

meant he had no one to look out for him when things went wrong. Luckily, on this occasion his plight attracted the attention of Oona, a feisty eight-year-old, who was nicknamed "the Needle," because she always carried one and was not afraid to use it. Seeing Thonir in trouble, she ran up behind the cooper and gave him a quick jab in the hock, the hollow behind the knee. The man bellowed, as his knee buckled, enabling the boy to break away and make a run for it, while Oona melted back into the crowd.

After making his escape, Thonir turned his attention briefly to the execution, as it continued on its gruesome course. He sensed the mood of the crowd splitting between those who were impressed and moved by Chodros's apparent stoicism and those who were disappointed and bored by it. The executioner sensed it, too, and—notwithstanding his earlier determination to show no mercy to an unrepentant criminal—began to side with those now calling for a quick end for the brave wizard. At the same time, he worried that the others might riot if the performance failed to live up to their exacting standards. He therefore made a great show of continuing to extract the remaining lengths of bowel, long after he had signaled for his assistant to pierce Chodros's heart with a metal skewer.

Thonir did not know whether his dour former master had actually been guilty of conspiring to kill the duke. He thought it unlikely, but not outside the realm of possibility. He was certain, however, that the wizard's late manservant and housekeeper had both been innocent. Whatever villainy Chodros might have been involved in himself, he would never have trusted his two servants sufficiently to include them. The boy spat angrily on the ground. The manservant he had never liked, but the housekeeper had been perhaps his only friend in the world, and in the end he had let her down.

Somehow the thought prompted him to spend two Mindoric farthings on a pocketful of fresh strawberries as a thank-you gift for Oona.

2

Gangs of homeless juveniles—often organized and exploited by a predatory adult, or "kidsman"—began to appear in the larger cities by the late medieval period. They typically engaged in begging, picking pockets, petty larceny, and in some cases prostitution.

— *Crime and Punishment in Medieval Ondiran*

Evidently Thonir had misjudged how much Dob expected him to bring in.

"'Tain't much for an execution," the kidsman grumbled. "You ain't holdin' out on me, are you, boy?"

Thonir hastened to deny any such thing. "It just wasn't a very good crowd, boss," he insisted. "Rich folk don't come out to the Bloodstone unless it's for one of their own. You told me that yourself."

Oraminta smirked at her pickpocketing partner and boyfriend, a thuggish seventeen-year-old known as "Pink" to his face and "Puke" behind his back. "We did all right," she pointed out. "I bet Magic-Boy *is* holding out on you, Dob."

Thonir shot her a poisonous look. She might be pretty, with a body that haunted his hormonal adolescent dreams, but he had realized early on that she was the worst of Dob's generally bad lot—though Puke came in a close second.

"Thon knows better than that, boss," objected a painfully thin fifteen-year-old named Ksol, a talented burglar whom Thonir had come tentatively to consider a friend. "Me and Fats had a shitty day, too."

"Shut up, Wormy," said Puke, giving the smaller boy a shove that sent him sprawling onto the packed-dirt floor of the warehouse. He evidently felt he could do so with impunity, as Dob generally turned a blind eye to his misdeeds. "Nobody cares what you think."

Dob rapped his walking stick impatiently on an old wooden crate. "Empty your pockets," he told Thonir. "Now!"

With a sorrowful glance at Oona, Thonir produced the strawberries. "These didn't come out of my takings, boss," he insisted, hoping for mitigation. "I stole them from a fruit vendor on the way back. Honest!"

"Either way, what you steal belongs to *me,* boy!" Dob confiscated the berries but refrained from striking Thonir with the walking stick, as he likely would have done with any of his other miscreants. He knew enough to be wary of the fledgling wizard's mystical powers. "Now get out of my sight!"

Thonir gave Ksol a hand getting up from the floor. Then, with what little dignity they could muster, the two slunk out of the warehouse and into the street.

Adapting to life in Dob's crew had been a process. The other children were all conversant with the Mindoric underworld's folkways, including its thieves' cant and secret sign-language. Although Thonir was a quick study, his initial ignorance of these things, coupled with his educated way of speaking, made him the object of a certain amount of ridicule. Although he was used to that from Chodros, he still found it humiliating.

Fortunately, after their painful initial encounter on the street, Puke and his chief cronies—a pair of fifteen-year-olds known as "Grub" and "Scrod"—were sufficiently leery of "Magic-Boy" to leave him largely alone. All three were beefy, muscular youths, however—having helped themselves, over the years, to more than their fair share of the food—and Thonir, to his shame, could not summon the courage to defend the other children from their predations. The three could so easily catch him unawares, if they chose to, especially at night. Thonir did not have enough enchanted chalk to draw protective circles around his patch of floor on an on-going basis, and "sleeping with one eye open" remained for him a mere metaphor rather than something he could actually do (though he had heard there was a wizarding spell to accomplish it). Admittedly, he was a little more successful in thwarting the abuses of the trio's obnoxious hanger-on, "Slinker," a ten-year-old bully-boy in training, who curried favor with them by terrorizing the younger children.

Oraminta, the only member of Puke's clique with any brains, ruled over the girls in the warehouse with subtle skill, keeping them quarreling, divided, and cowed (apart from Oona the Needle—no one except Dob himself had the slightest control over that one). Oraminta also did her best to encourage Puke's worst instincts, for his propensity to violence aroused and excited her. For some reason she also seemed to enjoy teasing and vexing Thonir, much to his annoyance.

With regard to some of the other teenagers, Thonir got along well enough with Ksol ("Wormy") and Porg ("Fats"). Thonir was quite sure Ksol did in fact suffer from worms, and he felt guilty for having failed to memorize the simple spell to banish them that Chodros had taught him and that now resided, unreachable, among the notes confiscated by the city watch. In contrast to the skinny Ksol, Porg was unique in Dob's gang for having somehow put on the weight one might have expected of a fashionable lady at the ducal court. In any event, the two shared a ravenous appetite for food and devoted a great deal of ingenuity to stealing enough to sate it, sometimes with Thonir's assistance, for he could cast spells to befuddle vendors at market and render them easy marks.

There were fewer girls than boys in the gang, and they were mostly in Oraminta's thrall, one way or another. The older ones followed her lead in looking to make trouble for Thonir, who tried—not very successfully—to ignore them.

The younger children Thonir regarded as a largely un-differentiated mob, with the exception of a few notable personalities like Slinker and the Needle. Another was a persistent nine-year-old who pestered Thonir to teach him wizardry. An experienced magician gains the ability to detect magical power in others, and Thonir was advanced enough to sense that this boy possessed very little.

All told, the inhabitants of the warehouse numbered twenty-three, including Dob himself, who lived in what had once been the warehouse manager's office, where he had an actual bed and a small but efficient woodstove that kept the room comfortably warm. The children dwelled in the main part of the warehouse, which was cavernous, drafty, and cold, notwithstanding the derelict old stove set up in one corner, flanked by two rickety double bunk-beds, one on each wall. Oraminta and Puke took the one on the left, Grub and Scrod the one on the right. Most of the other children had to make do with the floor—their proximity to the stove being determined by their size and ferocity—although a couple of the bolder spirits had rigged up hammocks far above, near the rafters, to take advantage of the rising warm air.

Thonir was glad to have the woolen blanket he had brought with him, as well as the sack of spare clothes he used as a pillow. Not everyone was so lucky. Being accustomed, however, to a room of his own—spartan though it had been—he disliked living in close quarters with so many other people. The fetid air in the warehouse reeked, reminding him of the cage in which he had kept a pet ferret when a small boy. Worse yet, by his second day with the gang, Thonir had fleas, by his fourth, lice. He berated himself for not having memorized the spell Chodros had taught him that would have exterminated these bloodsuckers, but at the time it had not seemed nearly so important as it did now.

3

Belief in magic was widespread in the medieval period. Indeed, purported magicians adhered to several competing schools. Those professing sorcery were most prevalent in Ondiran and Tserenets, wizardry in Esdiron and Iniroch, thaumaturgy in the lands further west.

— *The Encyclopædia Ondiricana* (12th ed.)

"Damn," said Thonir, as he and his skinny friend retreated from the warehouse in disgrace. "I'm sorry, Ksol. I shouldn't let Puke push you around like that."

Ksol rubbed his bruised buttock philosophically. Being so thin, he had very little padding. "That's all right," he said. "He's a big, mean bastard. Someday he'll come to a big, mean end. I just hope I'm there to see it."

They turned onto a street particularly favored by the port's large colony of seagulls, whose droppings were everywhere. Looking up, Thonir confirmed that several dozen of the birds were perched on the roofs above, while others swooped and wheeled through the air overhead, crying and squawking. Fats had told him that Ksol was partial to seagull eggs and sometimes risked his neck climbing up to raid their nests. It was a tricky business, because angry gulls could deliver some nasty pecks, but Ksol knew what he was doing and rarely came away bloodied.

The boy seemed to read Thonir's thoughts. "Naw," he said. "Too early in the year. They ain't nestin' yet. Besides, nighttime's better for stealin' eggs."

Passing into a less guano-encrusted street, they encountered a wiry youth with long, straw-colored hair and a sly expression.

"Hoi, Wormy," he said, nodding. "Thon."

"Hoi, Wheezer," they replied.

A former member of Dob's gang, "Wheezer" was now running with an older crew, but he and Ksol remained friendly. "Dob still feedin' you that pig-swill he calls food?" he asked (for Wheezer and Dob, by contrast, had *not* parted on good terms).

Ksol grunted noncommittally. Finding the quantities of food he needed to sustain both himself and his parasites took precedence over concerns about quality.

"Hey, listen, Wormy," Wheezer suggested. "Orco just nabbed us a coupla fat hens. Help us pluck 'em, and I bet Striker'll let you have the feet." ("Striker," Thonir knew, was the experienced thief who commanded Wheezer's crew. Who "Orco" might be, apart from a chicken-thief, and where he had gotten such an odd nickname, Thonir had no idea.)

Ksol's eyes lit up. "Hey, thanks, Wheezer!" He hesitated a moment. "D'ya think Thon could come, too?"

Wheezer turned to Thonir. "Sorry, Thon. Striker don't know you. I don't think he'll be too happy if I start bringin' in strangers."

Thonir shook his head. He was in no mood for socializing anyway. Or subsisting on chicken feet, of all things. "No, problem, Wheeze. I'm not looking to get you into any trouble." He and Ksol bumped fists in an underworld fare-well salute. "See you back at the warehouse."

Thonir's training in the arts of thievery had seen mixed results. Always a bit clumsy, he had shown embarrassingly little aptitude for picking pockets. In one recent test, six of the other children had been blindfolded and given coin purses, which he was then supposed to "lift" unnoticed. All six had easily detected his fumbling efforts. Indeed, when he tried to pick Grub's pocket, the boy had grabbed his wrist and twisted his arm nearly out of its socket, to hoots of laughter from the other children. Admittedly, Thonir had the last laugh when Grub mysteriously wet the bed that night. He knew there were other, more important spells he should have committed to memory back when he had the chance, but under the circumstances he was glad to have had this one at his disposal.

To be sure, Thonir had proven himself better at picking locks than at picking pockets. While he could open most such mechanisms by magic, he had seen the advantage of learning how to do so by hand—which was fortunate, since Dob insisted upon it—and in the weeks since joining the gang Thonir had become quite proficient. Recognizing his facility, Dob had assisted him in fashioning his own set of delicate tools for the job, as well as in modifying his belt so they could be hidden in it. His inadequacy as a pick-pocket notwithstanding, Thonir was good with his hands, and he enjoyed practicing on the extensive set of locks Dob kept for that purpose.

After parting with Ksol, Thonir wandered moodily out onto the docks so he could look at the ships and dream about places that were not Mindor. Having grown up in the port city, he was accustomed to the salty smell of the sea, though he still objected to the reek of the fishing boats and their catch. Taking a seat atop an upright barrel, he counted twelve merchant ships in the harbor, seven from various Ondiric jurisdictions, three from the island of Tserenets to the east, and two from the kingdom of Esdiron to the southwest. He scratched at a flea. There were wizards to be found in Esdiron, he reflected, but the place was alarmingly far away, and Chodros had not taught him as much Esdiric as he would have liked. Knowing how to call someone a "worthless arse-faced rodent-boy" or a "runty toad-brained coprophage" seemed likely to be of limited practical value were he to visit the country.

He sighed, watching as a pack of rats promenaded boldly down the wharf. Rats, fleas, lice—there had been no cause for him to worry about such afflictions while he lived with Chodros. Thonir was feeling sorry for himself, with—he believed—every justification. His old master was dead, his new boss was cross with him, and he was infested with vermin. Plus, he would probably be going without lunch today.

He had been brooding in this vein for some time when a three-masted carrack sailed into the harbor. Having seen one of these magnificent vessels only twice before, he sat up straighter and paid heed. Larger than the usual cogs, hulks, and caravels, this ship, with its four sails—including a lateen on the mizzenmast—was the pinnacle of current maritime technology. No Ondiric shipwright could have built it, and indeed it flew the flag of the Merchant Republic of Traak, one of the Inirochian city states that lay to the southwest of Esdiron. Thonir got off his barrel and approached for a closer look as the carrack docked.

The ship's captain seemed to be in a hurry. Barking orders in Inirochian, he soon had his ethnically diverse crewmen offloading crates and bundles with the help of the local dockworkers, but what got Thonir's attention was the presence of a tall man, in a rust-colored cloak, who aided in the process by magically levitating wine barrels from the deck to the dock. Judging by his dark hair, high cheekbones, and olive skin, he was likely an Inirochian, certainly a southerner.

Thonir's pulse quickened. Had he found a wizard in need of an apprentice? He approached closer and watched the barrels descend. When, at length, the unloading was finished, he screwed up his courage and called out the conventional greeting from the mystical language of wizardry: *"Kholenakht!"*

The southern wizard looked down at him in surprise. His eyes narrowed suspiciously, but he returned the conventional wizarding reply: *"Dholenakht!"*

Thonir flushed, suddenly conscious of just how scruffy, ill-dressed, and dirty he was. He resisted the urgent need to scratch at another flea. "I am an apprentice who has lost his master," he declared in Ondiric, enunciating the words slowly and distinctly, for he had no idea how well, if at all, this southerner might speak the language.

An Esdiric sailor poked his head over the side. "Shood ya no go look for eem, den?" he suggested, prompting a thin ripple of laughter from those of his fellows who understood Ondiric. The Mindoric dockworkers ignored him, having little time for the Esdir and their feeble notions of humor.

The southern wizard frowned. "What of it?" he demanded of Thonir. His Ondiric was good, despite a noticeable Inirochian accent. "What concern of mine is this?"

The boy swallowed hard. "I seek a new master, Eminence. A wizard with the skill and knowledge to complete my training."

"And you think I am such a wizard?"

Thonir nodded. "That is my hope, Eminence. Wizards are few here in eastern Ondiran. It is a land of sorcerers."

The Inirochian strode down the gangplank and contemplated Thonir with a skeptical expression. He placed a hand on the boy's forehead. "Bah!" he exclaimed. "I sense little magic in you."

Thonir's shoulders drooped. "No, Eminence. You wouldn't. I used all my *silendras* this morning casting a difficult spell at high power." He spoke its name in the wizarding tongue.

The Inirochian raised his eyebrows. "That *is* a difficult spell," he admitted. "One I would not have expected a boy your age to have at his command." He shook his head. "But no, I have no need for an apprentice." He reached into his pocket and produced a Traakan copper coin worth about two Mindoric pennies. "Get yourself something to eat, my boy. I am sorry, but you will have to find your new master elsewhere."

Thonir took the money with mumbled thanks, feeling more discouraged than ever.

4

Hrintism was unique among the major Ondiric creeds in employing a calendar based on an eight-day week, rather than the seven-day one favored by most of its competitors (or the six-day week of the Ondiric Civic Calendar). Having to work seven days out of eight, rather than six days out of seven, was the cause of much grumbling among the faithful, but it may well have contributed to their disproportionate prosperity, especially when compared to the Zoorists, with their five-day week.

— Faith and Folly: Religion in Medieval Ondiran

Thonir had realized early that the most promising way to make himself useful to Dob was to help him plan and execute burglaries. Much of Chodros's activity as a working wizard had taken the form of security commissions: protecting the homes and businesses of the well-to-do from unwanted visitors. As Chodros's apprentice, Thonir had trained heavily in this magical specialty. He had assisted his master on the job and thus knew who had employed the wizard's services and how to disable his protections. For their part, Dob's crew sometimes dabbled in burglary, but they had to limit themselves to places that did not have enough worth stealing to justify paying for magical protections. Thonir's arrival changed that calculus.

❖

24

The boy organized his first job just ten days after joining the gang. Since the point of the exercise was merely to establish the viability of the scheme, Dob agreed to let him pass over richer pickings in favor of indulging his petty desire for revenge against the alchemist who had cheated him on the day of Chodros's arrest. The prize would be limited to the alchemist's cash box, for Dob had no wish to fence a haul of potentially dangerous ingredients or mysterious alchemical paraphernalia. As a result, Thonir could hold risks to a minimum by taking only one person with him. Dob assigned his premier burglar, which was how Thonir got to know Ksol. The skinny lad could squeeze through incredibly tight spaces, and his talent for climbing was useful for more things than raiding seagull nests.

Thonir was an observant boy, and he had noticed, when receiving change on past visits, that the alchemist's cash box always appeared to be at its fullest on the day before the man closed his shop for the Hrintic Day of Rest, and emptiest the morning after it, when he reopened, which suggested that he must extract the bulk of his takings at the end of each Hrintic week. Thonir therefore planned the burglary for the night before that.

"The usual way magicians secure a lock," he explained to Ksol, as they made their way through the dark streets toward their target, "is to enchant it to make the owner's key the only one that can open it without triggering an alarm or a trap, or both. Use a skeleton key, a lock-pick, an unlocking spell—doesn't matter—if you don't dispel the enchantment on the mechanism first, you're in trouble."

Ksol nodded. "Yeah, I've wondered 'bout that."

"Of course, the magician needs to come up with an enchantment that's hard to dispel," Thonir continued, as they neared the shop, "preferably one that's actually triggered if you try to dispel it. But he's also going to have his own counter spell—and I know Chodros's." Although the alchemist had wanted Chodros to scatter random traps inside the shop (and offered to provide powerful acids for the purpose), fortunately the wizard had managed to convince him that this would be unwise, as the danger of triggering them accidentally was too great.

The boys sneaked into the narrow alleyway behind the shop and approached the back door. Thonir hoarsely whispered Chodros's one-word counter spell, deactivating a trap that would otherwise have rendered him comatose for several hours, even as it set off a rousing alarm. He then recited an incantation to disengage the lock before pulling open the door and peering into the darkness of the shop's back room. He wrinkled his nose as harsh chemical fumes wafted out into the alley. His heart pounding, he cast a dim light spell on a small stick he had brought along in lieu of a wand, causing faint reflections to glint and dance on the multitude of beakers, jars, retorts, and other glassware filling the room. He swallowed hard. Although the boy had sometimes gotten into mischief as Chodros's apprentice, he had never done anything quite so dangerous as this.

Followed closely by Ksol, who brought the door silently closed behind them, he willed his reluctant feet to creep past all the clutter and through the low doorway opposite, into a short hallway with stairs leading up to the alchemist's living quarters, as well as down to the cellar. There both boys paused, listening closely for any hint of movement upstairs. At the end of the hallway was another door, but Thonir quickly established that the alchemist had failed to fasten its enchanted lock. Finding the hinges squeaky, he threw a quick spell to muffle them and entered the tiny shop's crowded front room without mishap. He stepped sideways over to the cash box, which was chained to a shelf beneath the sales counter. Crouching down, he repeated his previous magicks and safely unlocked the chain. He then gently freed the box and handed it to Ksol, who began to retrace their steps down the dark hall.

Thonir did not immediately follow. He had another reason for targeting the alchemist's shop: he had taken pity on one of the younger teenagers in Dob's gang, a girl cruelly but aptly nicknamed "Zits," whom Oraminta particularly disliked. Thonir had therefore promised to make her the magical ointment that had cleared up his own complexion two years earlier. To do so, he needed one particular magical herb. He knew the alchemist kept it in one of the ceramic jars arrayed upon the shelves behind the sales counter. Set- ting down his illuminated stick, Thonir opened the heavy jar and removed a few pungent, purplish leaves. He was putting back the lid, when Ksol, unable to proceed without light, hissed at him from the doorway. Startled, Thonir fumbled with the lid, which slipped from his fingers and fell to the tiled floor, where it shattered. He snatched up his illuminated stick, and the two boys raced like whippets down the hallway, through the back room, and out into the dark streets, leaving the alchemist to come thundering down- stairs in his nightshirt and find himself burgled.

It was not in Ksol's character to tell tales, and Thonir was grateful for his silence, when they returned to the warehouse and reported to Dob. Thonir performed the necessary magicks to open the cash box safely, liberating a small profusion of silver, copper, bronze, and brass coins worth a total of nearly three Mindoric gold ducats. Dob was pleased. "You may earn your keep yet, boy," he told Thonir, bestowing upon each of the burglars a copper groat, worth a third of a silver shilling. "Where else should we hit?"

Their next targets were more ambitious—first a goldsmith's shop, then a silversmith's—and Dob sent Puke along, as well, chiefly to provide another pair of hands to carry home the loot, but also to keep an eye on the other two in case they got ideas about skimming. Both heists went smoothly, yielding a generous haul of gold and silver ingots, along with a good deal of fine jewelry and fancy silver tableware that Dob fenced to a ship's captain he knew, who spirited it out of the city. On these occasions, each boy received a silver half-shilling. Thonir saved his earnings, while Ksol spent his on food, and Puke on drink.

After three successful heists, Thonir began to worry that word would be getting around that Chodros's security measures had been compromised, and it turned out that their fourth target, the city's largest brewery, had in fact added an enormous wolfhound to its workforce for that very reason. Grub and Scrod came along this time, with the assignment of rolling a barrel of beer back to the warehouse, but no sooner had they tipped one over onto its side and begun to roll it toward the door, than the dog lunged snarling out of the darkness and sank its fangs into Grub's thigh. The boy screamed and his attacker growled. Waving his arms and shouting, Scrod kicked the beast, which reluctantly released its grip on Grub. Barking fit to wake the dead—had there been any nearby—the dog launched itself at Scrod, who vaulted over the barrel, desperate to get away. Thonir, who had been busy with the brewery's substantial cash box, improvised by throwing his befuddling spell. He was not sure it would work on animals, but the dog fell silent, stopped trying to bite Scrod, and took on a confused expression. Puke then stepped forward and clubbed it on the head with the lead-filled sap he always carried, causing the dog to collapse senseless to the ground.

Fortunately for the burglars, the brewery was a large, proto-industrial establishment, with no one living above it, so there was no one to hear the screams or the barking. Nevertheless, the intruders hastily removed themselves, with Thonir and Ksol lugging the cash box between them, Puke and Scrod pushing the barrel of beer, and Grub limping along behind, bemoaning his savaged leg.

Back at the warehouse, Dob sprinkled a little beer on the wound as a disinfectant before bandaging it with a filthy rag. Puke tried to pin the blame for encountering the dog on Thonir, who stoutly denied that the brewery had any such animal in its employ when Chodros set up its security arrangements. Dob waved away the dispute as trivial. He awarded no coins to any of the burglars this time, however, stating that the beer represented their rightful due, though they were of course obliged to share it with the other occupants of the warehouse.

❧

Thonir continued to worry that Chodros's former clients would be seeking out alternative means of securing their premises, but Dob pressed him hard to come up with further heists all the same. The kidsman loved nothing more than money, and the burglars were bringing in goodly sums compared to their daylight work picking pockets. Against his better judgment, Thonir therefore proposed hitting a spice emporium, surmising that the owner, as an ethnic Se'erdoon from far to the west, might not have heard about the recent spate of burglaries from his Ondiric fellow merchants and would therefore be less likely to have revisited Chodros's wards against intruders. It was a reasonable supposition, even if it did happen to be wrong.

The job took place two nights after Chodros's execution. Grub's leg had become infected, so a sullen fourteen-year-old boy called "Twitch" took his place alongside Puke and Scrod, who would again accompany Thonir and Ksol. Bored and hoping for some excitement, Oraminta persuaded Dob to let her go, as well. Although Thonir was uneasy at taking such a crowd of people, Dob overruled him. Spices were extremely valuable, so the kidsman wanted a large team to maximize the take. He gave each burglar a large sack, with firm instructions to steal everything in sight. Their pay for the job, he emphasized, would depend on how much they brought back.

The six teenagers waited until well after midnight before setting out for the spice merchant's shop, which was located in Terifen, or Northgate, a wealthy neighborhood near the city's unimaginatively named Northern Gate. The expedition nearly came to grief while still in the dock district, however, when two members of the city watch (or "bulls" in the underworld slang), crossed their path from a side street, carrying truncheons (or "bulls' pizzles"). From his lead position, Thonir heard their approaching footfalls before the men stepped into view some six yards ahead, and he dropped into a crouch, while urgently flashing the underworld hand signal telling the others to freeze. Distracted by Oraminta, whose shapely contours they had been ogling from their strategic position at the rear of the group, Scrod and Twitch were slow to comply and nearly compromised the operation. Luckily the night was dark, with only the smaller of the two moons at all in evidence, and the watchmen were enjoying a crude joke about their commanding officer, so the moment of danger passed without anyone coming to harm.

Thonir swore under his breath. "That was close," he whispered to the others. "Let's split up into pairs and go by different routes. I'm guessing the bulls keep a closer eye on Terifen than just about anywhere else—apart from the duke's palace, that is." He gave Scrod and Twitch a scathing look before adding, "Better they catch just two of us than all six!"

Puke resented the fact that Dob had put Thonir in charge of these burglaries, but he could not think of a more cogent objection to this change in plan than a skeptical "I dunno."

Oraminta sometimes found Puke's stupidity trying. She pursed her lips. "Magic-Boy's right for once." She gestured contemptuously toward Scrod and Twitch. "We'll stand a better chance of getting there safe without these two pervs tagging along behind, beating their wangs."

The six thus split up. Thonir and Ksol reached the spice merchant's without incident. Puke and Oraminta arrived next, slightly out of breath—though whether from dodging watchmen or engaging in a quick sex act in a dark alley, Thonir chose not to ask. While waiting for Scrod and Twitch, he ventured out of the shadows to do some reconnaissance. The shop was located on a street corner, and he intended to use the side door, but the lock required careful investigation first. He cast a spell to determine if it was enchanted, but he used a variant form that—if so—would also reveal what type of magic had been used. To his deep chagrin, the lock glowed a faint blue instead of yellow, which told him that Chodros's wizardry had been dispelled and replaced with sorcery, presumably by Chodros's local competitor, the sorcerer Runifor, an intense, profane little man, whose skills, Thonir knew, Chodros had respected, even if the two men disliked one another.

Worried, the boy slipped back into the shadows across the street, where Scrod and Twitch had just arrived, giggling stupidly about he knew not what. "We're screwed," he whispered. "The lock's been re-enchanted by a sorcerer."

Puke made a face. "Dob'll be pissed if we don' come back wit' squat," he said in his monosyllabic way.

Oraminta looked skeptically at Thonir. "Well, what about it, Magic-Boy? This was s'posed to be a big score for us. Can you and your hocus-pocus save the day, or are you really as useless as you look?"

Thonir squirmed. His strong preference was to abandon the operation, but he *did* know a complex counter spell to knock out Runifor's enchantment, if Runifor's it was. Chodros had devised one in the course of his professional rivalry with the man. He had not seen fit to teach it to his apprentice, but Thonir had secretly copied it out all the same. And Puke was right about Dob being angry if he called off the job. Further, the opportunity to impress a pretty girl—even if she was a manipulative little snake—was a heady temptation for a sixteen-year-old boy. Thonir scratched his head, trying to reconcile these conflicting considerations. In the end, however, he lacked the courage to look like a coward. "Well, I can *try* to disarm the sorcerer's enchantments," he said, tamping down a sense of overwhelming folly and impending doom, "but I can't promise it'll work."

"You'll make it work," Ksol said encouragingly. "And if you don't, we kin still run like hell." He had evidently forgotten that springing a magical trap might well prevent them from running at all.

5

The crime of burglary was typically punished on the first offense by branding. Recidivists could expect to lose a hand, although the Duchies of Trandit and Trusilor favored deprivation of a foot.

— *Crime and Punishment in Medieval Ondiran*

Thonir crept back across the street to the side door. In the weeks since joining Dob's gang, he had made a point of memorizing everything in his remaining notes, so he had Chodros's spell to counter Runifor's enchantments ready. After glancing anxiously up and down the dark street, he recited the incantation. The lock made a slight hissing sound, which worried him, but a further spell detected no lingering magic. Palms sweating, he unlocked the door and gently pushed it open. After illuminating the stick he had with him, he took a look inside.

The door accessed the spice merchant's storeroom, which looked much as Thonir remembered it. On the left a curtained doorway led to the public portion of the shop, while on the right an exterior door led to an herb garden. Against the far wall was the staircase to the living quarters above. A trap door in the floor led to the cellar. Seeing nothing out of order, Thonir stepped cautiously inside and signaled for his fellow burglars to join him. Then he paused for a moment to inhale the gloriously mingled scents of peppercorns, cinnamon, and cloves, cardamom, cumin, and coriander, among a dozen other spices. The merchant had paid Chodros for his services partly in kind, and Thonir had fond memories of the wonderful meals that followed.

As they entered, Puke and Scrod produced stubby tallow candles, which Thonir lit with a wave of his hand. Oraminta and Ksol immediately began to fill their sacks with bundles of spices—labeled unhelpfully in Se'erdoonic—while Twitch pushed aside the curtain in the doorway leading to the shop's front room. Thonir crossed over to a heavily reinforced door under the stairs, which led to the closet-sized strong-room where he knew the spice merchant hoarded his gold. He was just beginning the task of dispelling the lock's defenses, when disaster struck. Twitch had found the spice merchant's cash box in the front room but failed to wait for Thonir to come and disarm its protections, stupidly seizing the box instead and attempting to stuff it into his sack. There was a scorching flash and a tremendous bang whose sheer sonic force triggered, in its turn, an identical trap on the strong-room door, so that everyone was temporarily blinded and deafened, regardless of where they stood. Twitch screamed in terror and dropped the cash box on his foot, while Thonir staggered backwards and crashed painfully into a table laden with spice bundles. The other burglars likewise flailed about helplessly. Puke and Scrod dropped their candles, one of which rolled over to a bundle of dried mugwort that slowly caught fire. After what seemed a frighteningly long time, but could not have been more than half a minute or so, the victims' sight began to return, albeit imperfectly at first. Hearing took longer, and several of the burglars found their balance temporarily impaired, as well, due to the disruption caused to the fluid in their inner ears.

They were far from recovered by the time the spice merchant, resplendent in his crimson silk pajamas, descended the stairs carrying a wrought-iron poker, followed by his two teenaged sons, less opulently attired for slumber in white cotton loincloths but wielding curved steel daggers. The trap's initial flash had been followed by a spell illuminating the ceiling, so they had no need to encumber themselves with lamps or candles. The spice merchant exclaimed something fierce-sounding in Se'erdoonic and dealt the still woozy Scrod a crushing blow to the skull. The burlier of the two sons grabbed Oraminta roughly by the wrist, but he had underestimated the girl, who responded by pulling a knife and stabbing him in the throat.

Ksol had his back turned when the traps were sprung, so his sight recovered somewhat more quickly than most of the others'. He tested the door to the herb garden. Providentially, it was unlocked. Turning to shout for Thonir, his eyes widened in horror, as amidst the chaos he saw the spice merchant's second son slash open Puke's abdomen, with exceptionally messy results. Ksol's gorge rose, as he steadied himself against the doorframe, but somehow he managed not to vomit.

For his part, Thonir had taken the worst of Runifor's trap, which had gone off in his face. For much longer than the others, he could see nothing at all. His ears still ringing, his brain reeling, he could eventually hear someone calling his name—faintly, as though from a great distance. As he struggled to get up, he found himself being half-dragged into the herb garden, where the cool night air helped bring him more fully to his senses. As sounds of melee continued to issue from the shop, his vision cleared sufficiently to perceive his rescuer investigating the eight-foot stone wall enclosing the garden.

"Shit!" Ksol muttered, as he discovered that pieces of broken glass studded the top of the obstacle. The skinny boy dumped the spices out of the sack he had somehow kept with him and positioned the rough fabric over the jagged shards. "C'mon, Thon," he urged. "We gotta get outta here!" He gave his friend a leg up, and Thonir clambered onto the wall, before rolling clumsily off the other side.

"Oof!" The boy had not hurt himself seriously, but Ksol would not be so lucky, for Runifor had enchanted the exterior surface of the garden wall to be as slippery as ice. This trick took Ksol by surprise, and despite his skill as a climber, his descent from the wall was precipitous. He landed awkwardly on one foot and gasped in pain. While not broken, his ankle was sprained badly enough that he needed Thonir's help to walk. Together they hastened away into the darkness, serenaded by the spice merchant's wife, who was screaming from an upstairs window: "Heelp! Thiebs, murther, rubbors! Fire!"

6

Found in a diaspora across many of the western lands, the Se'er-doon are said to be an industrious and frugal people. As they are particularly active in trade, their colorful garb and geometric tattoos are now increasingly to be seen in Ondiric ports. Their speech, like all western tongues, is strange and difficult to learn. They worship weird idols and fear a complex hierarchy of devils.

— An Historical, Geographical, and Oeconomical Dictionary,
Being an Instructive Miscellany of Information
Useful to a Man of Business

Despite their haste, the two boys had to be careful—not least because their senses were still impaired. They only narrowly avoided a squad of eight watchmen headed for the spice merchant's shop. Given Ksol's ankle, the going was hard, so once they had cleared Terifen, they stopped to rest in a back alley. To hear one another over the residual ringing in their ears, they spoke louder than was really advisable, though neither was fully aware of it.

"Damn," said Thonir, who was still seeing faintly glowing afterimages. "I thought we were done for. Thanks for getting me out of there, Ksol."

The other boy probed his injured ankle gingerly. "We both got each other outta there. I don't think anybody else got away, though, d'you?" He shuddered. "I know Puke didn't. One of those western boys sliced his belly right open."

He shook his head. "I've been waitin' a long time to see that stupid bastard get his, but turns out it wasn't such a treat to watch after all."

Remembering the mechanics of Chodros's execution two days earlier, Thonir grimaced. He also made a decision. "I've had enough," he said. "I'm leaving Dob, and I'm leaving Mindor. You should, too, Ksol. Whoever didn't end up dead back there is going to squeal, for sure, and the bulls will be knocking down Dob's door before you know it."

Ksol considered this unattractive prospect for a moment. "I can't leave Mindor," he concluded sadly. "I got nothin', and I don't know noplace else. Maybe Wheezer kin talk Striker into takin' me on. Fats, too, I hope. Worth a try, anyhow."

Nursing a fierce headache, Thonir massaged his temples. "We've got to go back to the warehouse, though," he said, "to get our stuff and warn the others. Of course Dob will blame me for the whole fiasco, but as far as I'm concerned, he can rot in one of the grislier depths of hell. I told him this was getting too dangerous."

Ksol nodded. "Fiasco," he repeated to himself. It was not the first interesting new word he had learned since meeting Thonir. He shivered. "It's cold tonight. Let's get movin' again."

⁂

As they approached the dock district, the boys had an unpleasant encounter with a group of young toughs, who seemed to think that four-against-two would make for amusing odds, especially when one of the two was hindered by a

39

twisted ankle. Thonir managed to discourage them by setting the lead tough's hair on fire, but it was a close-run thing.

When they got to the warehouse, everyone was asleep
except for Dob, who was awaiting their return with great
impatience. "What happened?" he demanded, as Thonir
helped Ksol hobble over to a crate and sit down.

"The whole thing went straight into the crapper,"
Thonir replied bluntly. His necessarily hazy explanation of
the details did nothing to reassure the tetchy kidsman, who
immediately perceived the danger to himself as the salient
point.

"Damnation!" Dob shouted, banging his walking stick
on Ksol's crate and waking several sleepers. "You stupid
brats'll be the death of me!"

Ksol blanched. "It wasn't our fault, boss! Thon got us
into the shop just fine. It must've been one of the others
that tripped the trap."

Dob continued to channel his fear into rage. "Don't
talk back to me, boy!" he ranted, giving Ksol a hard knock
with his stick. He turned to Thonir. "And as for you, you
lackwit wannabe wizard . . ."

Thonir felt his own surging rage overcome his fear of
Dob. Although his *silendras* was low after an exhausting
night of spellcasting and trauma, the boy still had enough
power to slam the kidsman into the wall with a single guttural syllable coupled with a motion of his hand. "I warned
you," he shouted. "I told you it was too risky, but you were
too greedy to listen." Everyone was wide awake now. He
turned to face them. "Listen to me, all of you. The jig is up!
If Dob thinks he knows somewhere safe, make him take

you there. Otherwise, you'd better scatter before the bulls get here, swinging their pizzles at everyone in sight."

Pandemonium erupted. Some of the younger children began to wail, while the older ones besieged Dob, demanding to know if he had a safer place to hide them. Thonir walked disgustedly over to his small collection of belongings. With a gesture, he dispelled the protective chalk circle he had drawn around them and then gathered them up. He said a sad goodbye to Ksol and Fats, gave a nod to Oona, who was bundling up her own few belongings, and stepped out into the night.

7

One of the four major eastern religions, Asardianism is based on scriptures attributed to the ancient theologian and mystic Asardius, who posited a triad of deities: one benevolent, one malign, and one indifferent. According to Asardius, the first of these is the most worshipped but the least followed, the third garners little devotion yet exercises the greatest influence over human affairs, while the second occupies a middle position in both respects.

— *The Encyclopædia Ondiricana* (12th ed.)

Thonir needed a place to hide—and with luck, to sleep—until sunup. He chose the Asardian temple in which he had gathered his thoughts on the day Chodros was arrested. It was not far, he was sure he could handle the lock, and if the priestess found him in the morning, she was unlikely to beat him or have him arrested. She might even give him a bowl of porridge.

Once inside, he stretched out under his blanket on one of the pews, but despite his exhaustion, sleep did not come easily. His mind was too perturbed by the night's events, which he could not even reconstruct properly, given the impaired state of his senses at the key juncture. From what Ksol said, he knew that Puke could hardly have survived, but what had happened to Oraminta, Scrod, and Twitch? And who had tripped the trap? He did not think he had done so himself, but could he really be sure? He also had to wonder what would happen to the other denizens of Dob's warehouse. And was not this entire mess his own fault—first, for failing to stand up to Dob beforehand, and then, for failing to stand up to Oraminta outside the shop?

His parents had done their best to raise him in the Asardian faith, and he had clung to its ethical and moral precepts, even as he drifted away from its theological tenets under the influence of Chodros, who maintained that all religion was a snare and a delusion. He already had an uneasy conscience regarding his recent career in property crime, but what if he now shared moral responsibility for one or more deaths, as well? For the floggings and brandings that would likely be upcoming attractions on the Bloodstone?

Plagued by these restless thoughts, Thonir groaned. He rearranged himself on the narrow hardwood pew and tugged his blanket tighter to ward off the damp chill of the unheated temple. In his own defense, he submitted that Dob was the one chiefly to blame for it all. The greedy bastard. He recalled the way the angry kidsman had struck Ksol with his walking stick. Greedy *and* cruel. No, if the demons of Asardian cosmology were real, they were welcome to him. The boy stared gloomily up at the temple's vaulted ceiling. Contemplating further the paradox that was Dob, he did have to concede that the man was not all bad. Where Chodros had unfailingly found fault with his pupil, Dob had known when to encourage and when to praise. More puzzlingly, for all his avarice, he had never sold any of the girls to a brothel-keeper—or any of the boys, for that matter. And whatever his own carnal needs may have been, he apparently satisfied them elsewhere. Villain he might be, monster he was not.

Unable to sleep, Thonir got up and went out into the small courtyard behind the temple. He drank some water from the well on the far side of the courtyard and looked up at the stars, picking out the constellations of Crona the Cow and Favitol the Savage Rooster. He sighed, thinking of his father, who had told him the Ondiric folk tales in which these characters featured. Thonir's father had been a kind-hearted man, with a warm smile and humorous brown eyes, while his mother was more reserved, slower to laugh, and he had always found the emotions behind her colder blue eyes more difficult to read.

Returning to his pew, Thonir crawled back under his blanket. He was sorry he had not tried to persuade Ksol to quit Mindor along with him, for the young thief had proved to be a true friend. The boy shuddered, knowing that but for Ksol's help, he would surely be cowering in a dungeon cell by now, awaiting the convenience of Master Tor, the city headsman and judicial torturer—and possibly nursing a few grievous wounds, as well, courtesy of the spice merchant and his sons. He doubted Ksol would ever leave the city on his own, while he himself could never expect to return, being wanted both as a condemned traitor's apprentice and now as the magical mastermind behind a string of costly burglaries. It was therefore most improbable that they would ever meet again. And Thonir had learned long ago that real life was not like Ondiric folk tales, in which the improbable happened as a matter of course.

An iron tiredness crept over the boy. In the morning, he would have to find a ship ready to leave port, whose captain was willing to take on a scruffy, flea-bitten passenger with little money, but right now his thoughts were becoming increasingly disordered and dreamlike, until finally he drifted into an uneasy sleep.

Chodros's arrest may have cast Thonir into the gutter, but leaving Dob's warehouse had been his first step out. He had no inkling of how long and arduous the remaining climb was yet to be.

8

The ducal city of Mindor has long been Ondiran's most important port. Apart from a few charming late-medieval structures in the Old Town, the city is of interest chiefly for its modernity and bustle. Visitors should not miss the opportunity to admire the powerful battle fleet that docks in its deepwater harbor.

— The Motor-Tourist's Guide to Ondiran (2nd ed.)

Thonir awoke with a start. A young man wearing the gray robes of an Asardian sub-priest was shaking him gently by the shoulder, as the first light of dawn filtered through the long, narrow windows of the temple.

"Get up, my boy. I'm sorry, but you can't sleep here."

Thonir scrambled to sit up, as his brain jolted back into a wary wakefulness. He had gotten no more than two hours of sleep, and it felt like less. His eyes were dry, there was an unpleasant taste in his mouth, and he doubted he had recovered enough *silendras* to light a candle. "Um, sorry, Your Humility," he muttered, careful to give the sub-priest his correct form of address. "It was cold out there."

The sub-priest nodded. "Yes, I expect it was." He ran a hand over his shaven pate. "Well, no harm done, I suppose. You don't seem to have damaged the lock getting in." A faint smile played at the corners of his mouth. "Still, you'd best be on your way before Her Serenity, Priestess Srogilte, gets here. She can be a bit testy first thing in the morning. What's your name, anyway?"

"Fenith," replied Thonir, as he rolled up his blanket.

"Sub-Priest Videril." He looked at the boy critically. "You must be hungry."

Thonir nodded. He was, very.

Videril somewhat reluctantly produced the bread roll that was to have been his own breakfast. "I suppose you'd better have this, then."

Thonir took it. "Thank you."

The sub-priest made the Asardian sign of benediction. "Bless you, Fenith," he said in the ancient Gantelic speech of the Asardian liturgy, adding in Ondiric, with an unexpected nod to ecumenism, "Go with whatever gods you believe in."

After devouring the bread roll, Thonir washed as best he could in the public fountain on a nearby square, after which he exchanged his urchin's rags for the spare clothes in his sack. They hung loosely on him, for he had lost weight since last he wore them. Shivering in the morning chill, he assessed the state of his finances. In addition to the copper groat and two silver half-shillings Dob had paid him for the burglaries, and the Traakan copper the Inirochian wizard had given him on the docks, he had a Mindoric copper penny and three brass farthings, a Fendoric tin half-farthing, and a Tseren copper *tüzen,* all of which, taken together, he calculated, amounted to about a shilling and two-thirds, maybe a little more, depending on how much the Traakan and Tseren coppers were actually worth. For someone long accustomed to reckoning his net worth in pennies, it seemed a goodly sum, but he knew it would not last a traveler long.

⚜

Thonir reached the docks just as they were coming alive with the activity of the new day. He counted eleven merchant ships of varying types and sizes, alongside innumerable fishing boats and other small craft of no use to him. He decided to begin with a sturdy cog flying the red dragon flag of the Duchy of Hriss, in the hope that it was headed homeward. The crew appeared to be engaged in ordinary maintenance, apart from two sailors on the wharf, who were arguing about vegetables, of all things. Thonir approached and wished them a good morning.

The first sailor gave him a bored nod.

"Onions," scoffed the second. "Sure, if you want yer breath to stink like seepin' pus!"

The first sailor shook his head. "Not if ya cook 'em right, Rilf. My Gheta cooks onions so good 'n' sweet—fit for the duke hisself, they are!" He took a second look at Thonir. "What is it, kid? Whaddaya want here?"

Thonir stood a little straighter. "I'm trying to get to Hriss. Are you bound for there?"

The first sailor shook his head. "Nah, not yet. We're headed north, to Vildenon—leastwise, once this wind shifts."

The second sailor spat. "Five days we been stuck in this shithole, waitin' on the damn wind."

The first one laughed. "You're just mad cuz ya diced away yer pay first night. Ain't nothin' wrong with sittin' in port so long's ya got money for whores."

Seeing nothing to be gained from prolonging this charmless encounter, Thonir bade the two sailors good day and headed instead for a prosperous-looking hulk flying the gold-green-and-white tricolor of the northern Duchy of Trusilor. The crew was busy loading cargo. Two imposing men, whom Thonir rightly took to be the captain and the ship's mate, were talking with a well-dressed merchant on the wharf. Thonir waited at a discreet distance until they had completed their business, then approached with the same query about their intended destination.

The captain, a large, rugged man with a coarse beard, looked at Thonir with vague annoyance. "Esdiron, with stops on the way." He rolled the *r* in "Esdiron" in the northern manner. "What of it?"

"When do you set sail?" Thonir asked.

"Soon as these lazy louts get the cargo loaded." He raised his voice to a harsh shout. "Move it, you damned tortoises! If we miss the tide—" He left the threat unspoken, but Thonir was sure it was not an idle one.

"How much to take me to Hriss? I can work."

Both men laughed. "Work can you, boy?" sneered the captain. "Then show me your calluses. Those hands look pretty soft to me. Soft as a girl's."

"That they do," chortled the ship's mate, "but don't forget, Cap'n, girls have their uses, too. Mind you, most girls is prettier than this kid."

Thonir flushed angrily. But for his lack of *silendras,* he would gladly have given both men a magic push off the wharf into the harbor. "Never mind!" he told them. "I'll find my passage elsewhere."

Their mocking laughter followed his retreat. "Who cut your hair, boy?" the ship's mate called after him. "Ye gods, I've seen *sheep* better shorn!"

※

Thonir had no more success at the next three vessels he approached, and he was starting to feel discouraged, when he arrived at a trim two-masted caravel called the *Porpoise*, which flew the gold-and-white flag of Vildenon, the empire's theoretical capital. The crew was just finishing the task of loading their cargo, and the captain, a short, wiry, weather-beaten man in his mid-forties, proved willing to take on a paying passenger who offered to work in exchange for a reduced fare. The ship's first port of call was the city of Karandoz on the island of Tserenets, but the captain stated his intention of proceeding thence to Risdar and Hriss. They agreed on a Mindoric groat for each leg of this journey, and thus a silver shilling for "Fenith" (as he deemed it safer to continue calling himself for now) to travel all the way to Hriss.

Taking advantage of the turning tide, the crew of the *Porpoise* cast off and raised the craft's elegant lateen sails almost as soon as Thonir came aboard. The captain assigned the youngest member of the crew, a lanky seventeen-year-old named Vort, to get their passenger settled. Thonir was relieved that the boy was disposed to be friendly, for he himself was too exhausted—both physically and magically— to cope with a bully, especially before getting his sea legs.

Eager to show off the *Porpoise,* Vort praised the vessel's speed and maneuverability with proprietary pride. "There ain't many pirates could catch us," he boasted, "specially if they can't beat to windward like we can."

Thonir nodded, fully aware of the advantages of the caravel's nimble triangular sails. Indeed, as a boy who had grown up in a port city, he could see that the *Porpoise* was impressively well designed and built.

"I'm tellin' you, Fen," Vort continued, "you won't find a better crew than ours, neither. My Uncle Vortan's a right smart captain, and he knows how to pick 'em."

Thonir replied tactfully that he was glad to hear it.

Vort seemed to think that coming from the imperial capital did himself almost as much credit as serving on such a fine ship. "Mindor's all right," he acknowledged generously, as they went below decks, "but Vildenon's the real deal. Sure, maybe the emperor ain't up to scratch, but he's got himself a right grand capital!" He went on at length regarding Vildenon's manifold advantages, one of which, he claimed, was having the prettiest girls in all Ondiran.

When the boys returned topside, the boatswain ordered them to get busy stowing miscellaneous gear cluttering the deck. As they worked, Vort continued to have a great deal to say on a wide variety of topics. Not everything he said was strictly true, but Thonir was shrewd enough not to believe everything he heard. Among other things, however, he did learn that Captain Vortan operated as a free agent. Not only did the man own the *Porpoise* outright, but after years of hauling cargo for other people, he had accumulated enough capital to start buying and selling goods on his own account. For the current journey, he had purchased a load of tin someone had brought downriver from the mines in southern

Fendoran, and Vort expressed confidence that it would fetch a good price in tin-poor Tserenets. "Buy low, sell high—that's how Uncle Vortan does it!"

Lunch consisted of dried fish, black bread, and cucumber pickles, washed down by a harsh liquor. Thonir welcomed the nourishment, but the alcohol in particular did nothing to alleviate the light nausea he was experiencing from the unaccustomed motion of the ship. Soon he was also hit by a sudden, overwhelming wave of tiredness, as his lack of sleep caught up with him. He made his apologies and hastened below decks, where he slept for much of the afternoon. This much rest was not enough to restore his *silendras* fully, but it made a good start.

Supper brought dried fish and black bread again, this time served with an unfamiliar purplish root vegetable that Vort explained was native to the County of Risdar. "Cook always buys a shit-ton of 'em when we pass through there," he said. "Don' know what they're called, but they keep forever, and they really ain't so bad once you get used to 'em."

After eating, Thonir helped Vort with various nautical chores until it grew dark, at which point both boys retreated to their bunks, as did several of the older sailors. Thonir was tired, but he did not fall asleep right away, as he reflected with satisfaction on his successful escape from Mindor and with lingering guilt on the unknowable fate of those he had left behind.

He ultimately managed to get a good night's sleep, however, and woke feeling back to full strength at last. His mood did sag a bit when breakfast proved to consist of more dried fish and black bread (now somewhat stale), accompanied by a little pickled cabbage, but he vastly preferred it to going hungry and knew better than to complain.

Having followed the Ondiric coast the previous day and most of the night, the *Porpoise* had turned away from it shortly before dawn and was now crossing the wide channel that separated Ondiran from Tserenets. With Vort otherwise occupied, keeping watch from the crow's nest, Thonir climbed onto the forecastle, where an older sailor named Gril taught him how to tie a number of useful knots, while regaling him with stories of the sea monsters he claimed to have seen in his time, especially off the coasts of Esdiron and Hriss. "Aye, some monstrous strange things live in them warmer waters down south," Gril declared, "things you don't see much round these parts, thank the saints and prophets!"

Thonir was unsure how seriously to take these yarns. He knew sailors had a reputation for telling tall tales, but he also knew the sea held some fierce and terrible creatures. He had once seen a large shark some fishermen had brought in, and its teeth were the stuff of nightmares. All he could do was hope that he would never encounter anything like that himself.

Lunch was by this time a sadly predictable affair, but Thonir decided that Vort was right: the Risdaric root vegetables were tasty enough, once you got used to them. Fortunately, the weather continued to be excellent for sailing, with a stiff breeze and good visibility. Before long, the *Porpoise* was within sight of land, and as the mariners neared the Tseren coast, they were met by a flight of seagulls that swooped and squawked overhead for several minutes before departing. "They were hopin' we were fishermen," explained Vort, chuckling, "so they could raid our catch." He waved goodbye, as the disappointed gulls departed. "Tough luck!" he shouted cheerfully after them. "Damn birds," he added, less charitably, as he spotted some droppings they had left behind that he and Thonir would now have to clean up.

Thonir, who was familiar with the habits of gulls, smiled wryly as he reached for a mop. He would not have begrudged them a few stolen fish, had there been any to steal. After all, there was a certain symmetry with Ksol's raids on the gulls' nests of Mindor. Nothing incited man or bird to thievery quite like the pangs of hunger. Unfortunately, he could attest to the truth of that from his own experience

9

Karandoz is a busy modern port. Although the city has little of conventional tourist interest, the recently constructed university has become a beacon of youth counterculture. A number of hostels in its vicinity provide inexpensive accommodation.

— Tserenets on 10 Crowns a Day

Thonir moved up to the prow for a better view, as the *Porpoise* tacked past a long rocky promontory or headland into the large bay that sheltered the port of Karandoz. At the end of this headland stood a tall square tower built of reddish stone. Although Thonir had never seen a lighthouse before, he had heard of them and surmised that this structure probably served as one at night and as a watchtower during the day. Even from a distance, he could see that the city on the far side of the bay was large, with stout walls of that same reddish stone, which he found more attractive than the drab gray of Mindor's fortifications. In addition to the usual fishing boats, the harbor held at least a dozen ships of all shapes and sizes, flying flags of various jurisdictions, not all of which he could identify. The most impressive was a Traakan carrack—even larger than the one Thonir had recently seen in Mindor—that passed quite close to the *Porpoise* as it sailed out of the bay.

The crew expertly maneuvered the caravel into dock, and the captain disembarked. He spoke briefly on the wharf with some serious-faced men wearing the green-and-gold colors of Tserenets, whom Thonir took to be customs inspectors, and headed off into the city. Seeming to understand that they were expected to stay put, the crewmen busied themselves with routine tasks.

"The captain's off to see a broker who'll arrange to auction off our cargo," explained Vort. "Then he'll bring back wagons, and we'll unload the ship."

⚜

It was late afternoon before the captain returned, accompanied by wagons, just as Vort had predicted. "All right, men," he shouted from the wharf. "Let's get this tin shifted!"

Determined to make himself useful, Thonir approached the ship's mate. "I can help," he said. "I know magic, and I can get the tin up here on deck for you. That should save a lot of work."

The ship's mate looked skeptical but nodded. "That it would, kid. All right. Let's see what you can do."

Thonir uttered some guttural syllables in the wizarding tongue and levitated a forty-pound ingot through the cargo hatch and into the waiting hands of one of the crewmen, who hurried away to the gangplank with it.

"Hell's bells," said the ship's mate. "That'll do it, kid! Keep 'em comin'."

Vort's astonishment was palpable. "Holy shit, Fen!" he exclaimed. "You didn' tell me you were a sorcerer!"

"A wizard, actually," Thonir replied, pleased to have made an impression on the older—and up to now rather patronizing—boy. He levitated a second ingot up for Vort to carry away. "Well, an apprentice wizard, anyway."

As Thonir continued the job of delivering ingots to a line of waiting crewmen, the customs inspectors on the wharf weighed the first one, recorded the Tseren equivalent of forty Ondiric pounds in their ledger, and began keeping a tally as the crew loaded the tin onto the wagons. Occasionally they weighed another ingot as a spot check, but they did so less and less often when they kept getting the same result.

Over time, magicians learn to cast their spells ever more efficiently, using less and less magical power to achieve the same effects, but as a mere apprentice, Thonir had far to go in this regard. Levitating the heavy ingots therefore drained his *silendras* more quickly, and he was forced to quit with perhaps a quarter of the load still below.

The ship's mate gave him a friendly slap on the shoulder. "That's all right, kid. You sit down and take a rest. We'll manage."

Thonir wandered over to the ship's bulwarks and watched the crew load the wagons. He was getting hungry, but he was certain there would be no supper until the tin was safe in the broker's warehouse. Therefore, once the wagons were loaded, and the captain had paid the customs men the crown's excise, he tagged along and got his first look at the city.

Vort was a fount of information regarding almost everything they saw, though Thonir was unsure how much of it to believe. He seriously doubted, for example, that the priests at a rather ominous-looking temple they passed actually performed human sacrifice to mark midwinter, or that Vort was a favorite customer at one of the larger dockside brothels. Perhaps the boy was trying to make up ground he felt he had lost upon learning that Thonir could do magic, but he told his stories entertainingly, and Thonir sensed no malice in him.

When they arrived at the warehouse—a dingy building at the back of a large gated courtyard—Thonir did his best to pitch in, although a forty-pound ingot was definitely a heavier load than he was accustomed to carrying. By the time the job was done, his muscles ached and his stomach growled. Fortunately, since everyone else was just as hungry, they headed for a nearby tavern without delay. Thonir could not read the Tseren name, but from the vividly painted sign, he guessed it was something like "The Mad Bull."

The establishment was small, with a low ceiling and no windows. Dimly lit by flickering tallow candles and a crackling wood fire in a brick fireplace, it might even have been described as cozy, but for the rancid smell of burning tallow, which competed muscularly with the more pleasing aroma of roasted meat. The other customers were eating and drinking with a concentration Thonir thought boded well for the quality of the fare.

"The cook's an Ondir," Vort confided, "so we'll have somethin' nice." He made a face. "These Tseren are all right in their way, but they can't cook for squat."

The captain announced that the meal and everyone's first ale were on him. "That includes you, Fenith," he told Thonir. "You did good work today."

"Hear, hear!" seconded the ship's mate, and the crewmen rapped their knuckles on the tables in a form of applause.

Unaccustomed to being appreciated, Thonir blushed and looked down at his hands, but the arrival of the ale soon provided a distraction, as indeed did the waitress who brought it, for in addition to being young and attractive, she had the seemingly superhuman ability to carry ten tankards at a time. A cheerful lass, she said something in Tseren that made the captain and those few crewmen who understood it laugh. The ale itself Thonir found less appealing, for Tseren brewers favored an admixture of harsh herbs, coupled with a higher alcohol content, that gave it a bit of a bite. He decided that he preferred the smoother beers of Ondiran and thus reluctantly nursed the contents of his tankard for the rest of the evening rather than spend his own money to procure more of the stuff.

Fortunately, the food when it came was delectable—pork cutlets smothered in a rich mushroom gravy and sprinkled with chopped parsley, along with green beans and fresh brown bread. Thonir feasted, as did his companions. Listening to the captain talk with the ship's mate as he ate, he gathered that the broker had a small consignment of pig iron the captain thought would be worth picking up, but they would need to reach out to the captain's other commercial contacts to find more goods to fill out the cargo. Apparently, they could expect to spend at least two or three days in Karandoz, as a result.

After the meal, everyone shuffled back to the docks. Despite some grumbling about the quality of Tseren ale, few members of the crew had let their reservations stop them from consuming the foamy liquid in volume. Upon reaching the dockside brothels, several of the sailors took their leave of the company amidst some decidedly bawdy commentary. Thonir found the idea of joining them a simultaneously enticing and alarming one, but both his physical exhaustion and his financial precarity militated firmly against it. He was amused, however, that Vort, for all his earlier boasting, also demurred, pleading insufficient funds. Both boys therefore accompanied the remaining sailors back to the *Porpoise,* where they fell into their bunks and sadly contemplated what they were missing, until they fell asleep.

❦

Thonir woke late the next morning, only to find much of the crew either still asleep or badly hung-over. Vort was among the sleepers, moaning softly in his bunk, no doubt still dreaming of buxom prostitutes. Thonir got up and went topside, where he met the ship's mate, who had raided the galley for some dried fish and hardtack. The cook evidently had not yet returned from the brothel.

"Lazy bastard didn't buy any fresh bread yesterday," the mate grumbled, offering Thonir a slab of hardtack.

"Thanks." Thonir tried to bite into the alleged comestible. It defeated him. "Where's Captain Vortan?"

The mate shrugged. "He went out early to find us some cargo. That man don't let the grass grow under his feet."

Thonir put the hardtack in his pocket. He looked closely at the mate, who was in his mid-to-late thirties and notable for a sort of benign ugliness. "Vort says he knows his business."

The mate laughed. "Our boy Vort says a lotta things. He's right, though, in this case."

Spoken of, like the proverbial devil, in Vort walked, or rather, emerged from below decks and joined them. "Mornin'," he said, looking with distaste at the dried fish and hardtack. "Say, can me an' Fen go into town an' check out the market? I've had enough of this shit for breakfast!"

The mate laughed again. "Sure. You two go on. There's nothin' doin' here this mornin' with half the crew dead to the world and the other half still missin' in some stinkin' whorehouse."

❧

"The thing about the market," Vort explained, as he and Thonir proceeded down the gangplank, "it's a great place to meet girls!"

This sounded promising, and Thonir felt wonderfully refreshed in the brisk spring morning air, as the two boys strolled down the city's narrow streets toward its central marketplace. For a boy who had never left Mindor before, everything was new and exciting, and normally he would have had a lot of questions for Vort, but today the other boy had a lot of questions for him instead, about magic, and Thonir found that it was nice to do a little more of the talking for a change.

"Man alive!" Vort said enviously as they entered the market. "It must be great. I mean, you must know spells that'll make girls do anything you want!"

Thonir answered vaguely. Tempted though he had sometimes been to make such use of charm spells, he could not shake the conviction that to do so would be an inexcusable abuse of his powers. He wanted to think his parents had raised him better than that. Hell, even Chodros, hardly an ethical paragon, had warned him against it. But having no desire to get into an argument, he changed the subject.

The late-morning market was a veritable anthill of activity, though considerably noisier. Peasants from the countryside hawked their produce at full volume, while urban artisans sang out the virtues of their wares. Shoppers shouted questions, while a gang of unkempt beggar children screeched for alms.

Vort's eyes lit up, as he caught sight of something on the far side of the market square. "C'mon, Fen!" he shouted. "Let's check out the slave auction!" As they pushed their way through the crowd, he explained that slave girls were usually displayed half-naked. "They're mostly westerners," he admitted, "but they can be damn pretty, too, y'know."

Thonir knew that slavery—though legal everywhere—was more common in Tserenets and Esdiron than in Ondiran. Admittedly, he had heard that the serfs of central Ondiran lived little better than slaves, but he shared a distaste for human bondage that was widespread among the Ondir, particularly in the eastern sovereignties. As a sixteen-year-old boy, however, his interest in feminine anatomy was as intense as his first-hand knowledge of it was limited, and the voyeuristic prospect of bare flesh was unquestionably alluring. Keeping his ethical reservations to himself, he therefore followed Vort across the square to the set of manacles dangling from a pole that advertised the slave mart.

When they got there, however, it was clear that the auction was over, and all that remained were three lots that had attracted no bids. Two were young western boys, one a Se'erdoon, the other of some ethnicity Thonir did not recognize, but he could easily see why neither had sold. The Se'erdoon had an infected wound on his leg, while the other boy, who could not have been older than eight, appeared to have rickets. The third slave was an elderly Inirochian woman with cataracts, her sightless eyes a cloudy blue. The slavers, a pair of hard-looking southerners—probably Esdir, Thonir thought—were haranguing passers-by in a determined manner, hoping to offload the last of their merchandise. Thonir turned away. There was nothing he could do for these unfortunates, and he blushed with shame at having hoped for what he could now see would have been a thoroughly demeaning spectacle.

Vort appeared to have no such qualms. "Aw, shit, we missed it," he groused. "C'mon, Fen, let's go find us some breakfast!"

Vort's sharp eye for pretty girls quickly led them to a pair of flaxen-haired maids who were selling small but decidedly tempting honey cakes. Vort knew a little Tseren, as it turned out, and immediately began a flirtatious conversation that induced a good deal of giggling on the part of the two girls, who seemed happy to enter into the spirit of the thing. "The cakes cost eight *nemtek* apiece," he told Thonir at length. "That's two-thirds of a copper *tüzen*. I told them we'd buy four, two for us and two for them, so we need two *tüzentek,* and what, eight *nemtek?* I've got one *tüzen.* What've you got?"

Thonir produced his own *tüzen.* "This is the only Tseren money I have." He considered for a moment. "I've got three Mindoric farthings, though. That should make up the difference, more or less."

The girls conferred and decided that Thonir was due one *nem* in change. This turned out to be a small iron piece, slightly rusty and stamped with the image of a bird of some kind, which was probably meant to be an eagle but looked more like a wood pigeon.

The conversation continued as the four nibbled on their honey cakes. Vort paused only occasionally to translate. "They're sisters," he noted, something Thonir had already guessed based on the family resemblance. Vort indicated the older and prettier of the two. "That one's Notaz. The other's Linets. Their father's a baker, but they make the honey cakes themselves."

Thonir nodded and pointed at what was left of his. "They're very tasty."

Vort translated, and the girls smiled appreciatively. Vort continued speaking Tseren, and the girls gasped and looked wide-eyed at Thonir. "I told 'em you're a sorcerer," the boy explained. "I don' know the Tseren word for wizard."

Notaz seemed to think better of her initial credulous reaction. Crossing her arms, she said something in a skeptical tone.

"She says prove it," Vort said. "Do some magic."

Thonir thought for a moment. Chodros had emphasized practical spells in his instruction, not party tricks, and Thonir had generally tried to memorize the most useful magicks rather than the showiest ones. Most of these fell in the security realm, but he had no locks to enchant or traps to deactivate. Setting fire to something seemed like a bad idea, so he fell back on levitation, causing a honey cake to rise from the table and dance around Notaz's head.

The wide-eyed look returned to Notaz's pretty face, and Linets squealed delightedly, while Vort laughed and clapped his hands. "That showed her!" he exclaimed. Pleased, Thonir brought the honey cake back down to rest on the girls' market table, where Notaz picked it up and offered it to him by way of reward. He broke it carefully in half and shared it with her.

Perhaps a trifle miffed that Thonir seemed to be making such a hit with the older and prettier sister, Vort plunged back into his basic conversational Tseren. It was a difficult language, Thonir knew, and the girls were clearly impressed that Vort could speak it at all, even if his thick Ondiric accent made them giggle and he often struggled to find the word he needed.

After a long stretch of flirtatious and translation-free chatter, Vort finally turned to Thonir and told him: "I got 'em to agree to let us buy them supper tonight at the Black Dragon. I've been there before. It's a nice place."

Thonir nodded. "Well done, Vort!" He hesitated. "But where do you suppose we're going to get the money to pay for it?"

Somewhat later, as the two continued to prowl around the market, eying the occasional nice-looking woman who was clearly too old for them, a shabbily dressed boy of about thirteen bumped clumsily into Vort.

"Hey, watch it, arse-wipe!" exclaimed the latter reflexively in Ondiric.

Thonir's experience in Dob's gang, however, led his eye from the "bumper" to his accomplice, the "lifter," a skinny twelve-year-old, as the latter laid claim to Vort's coin purse and began to make tracks. "Pickpockets!" Thonir shouted. "Grab them!"

Evidently Vort knew something about wrestling, as he not only grabbed the "bumper," but slipped a foot behind him and threw him to the ground. At the same time, Thonir cast a spell and the "lifter" collapsed as he ran, collided with a fully laden donkey, and fell sprawling to the ground, where he began to snore.

Vort put his foot on the first boy's neck and said something menacing, in Tseren this time, while Thonir went over and recovered Vort's purse from the second boy, along with two more that clearly did not belong to him. Vort relieved the "bumper" of the few small coins in his pockets, gave him a good hard kick, and sent him on his way. "Thanks, Fen," he said fervently. "Lucky thing you spotted 'em, the thievin' bastards."

Thonir counted the money in the two confiscated purses. "Six of those iron coins—what did you call them, *nemtek?*

—plus five copper *tüzentek* and two little silver pieces. They must be *izgöttek,* right?"

Vort looked at the coins in question. "Sure nuff." He laughed. "Hey, Fen, you'll be speakin' Tseren 'fore you know it."

Thonir smiled. "More to the point, now we have a way to pay for supper."

❖

That evening at the Black Dragon, however, the boys were in for disappointment, as the two girls from the market failed to appear. Vort was most put out and only half-jokingly suggested that Thonir's hair might have scared them off. "I'm sorry, Fen, but you look just awful. You sure you ain't been lettin' a goat graze on yer head?"

Thonir reflected morosely that the girls had more likely thought better of trusting someone who might use magic to take advantage of them—not that they would have been crazy to distrust Vort, either. He sighed, realizing that the memory of Notaz's wide-eyed admiration might be all he had to sustain his erotic imagination for some nights to come.

The frustrated lotharios consoled themselves with a large meal, washed down with enough ale to get them both a little drunk. Even so, there was money left over, and if nothing else, Thonir ended the day a little less impoverished than he had started it.

10

Only the more adventurous motor-tourist should venture into the County of Risdar, with its bad roads and hilly terrain. Be sure to bring extra fuel cans, as petrol stations are few and far between!

— *The Motor-Tourist's Guide to Ondiran* (3rd ed.)

The next morning was a busy one. Captain Vortan had taken an advance from the broker against his shipment of tin and used it to buy the pig iron he wanted, along with three dozen truckles of Tseren cheese, all of which needed to be loaded onto the *Porpoise*. The pig iron came in ingots, or "pigs," weighing the equivalent of forty-six Ondiric pounds, and the truckles were nearly as heavy, so the sailors were happy to have magical help.

Vort breathed in the pungent aroma of the cheese with reverence, as he lugged a truckle up the gangplank. "The Tseren may not know how to cook," he told Thonir, as the boy levitated it down into the hold, "but they sure know how to make cheese!"

For their part, the customs men were just as attentive to the goods being exported as they had been to those imported two days earlier, diligently weighing, counting, and recording, until they finally assessed the duty Captain Vortan had to pay. "They're strict here in Tserenets," the ship's mate remarked to Thonir, "but the rate they charge ain't so bad, specially on exports. It's the Esdir who're the real bastards."

Once the ship was loaded, however, the crew had to wait until mid-afternoon for the tide to shift before casting off. In the meantime, Vort proposed that the cook, who doubled as the ship's barber-surgeon, should cut Thonir's hair, "so the girls don' think he's got mange or somethin'." Thonir was agreeable. In the weeks since he had cropped it with his penknife, his hair had grown out enough to give the cook something to work with, and he would far rather have the job done now in the calm of the harbor than with the ship pitching and rolling at sea.

The cook was a large man in his early thirties, with prominent gray eyes and a shaven head. He hailed from the Margravate of Ghendor, the westernmost province of Ondiran, bordering on the Central Steppe, and spoke an outlandish frontier dialect of Ondiric that seemed to Thonir to border on gibberish. Ghendor was hundreds of miles from the sea, and how this man had come to be a mariner was anyone's guess, but he knew how to handle a razor and owned an iron spring scissors, so no one questioned his authority to cut hair.

"Sidoon, kit," he told Thonir, once Vort had put the proposition to him and he had fetched his equipment, which included a small wooden crate.

Interpreting this as a request for him to take a seat on the crate, Thonir did so.

"Gah!" exclaimed the cook almost immediately. "Laos!" He showed Thonir the louse he had plucked from the boy's scalp. "Ifn ah feenah noother, we raysum." He placed the louse carefully in his coin purse and pulled the drawstrings tight, so it could not escape.

Vort gave an enthusiastic cry. "There's gonna be a louse race, fellas!"

Thonir had done his best to extirpate the little bloodsuckers by crushing the life out of them whenever he caught one, but he was not surprised that the cook eventually found another. By the time the haircut was finished, two crewmen had come forward with lice of their own, and the excitement of the impending race—with its attendant opportunity for gambling—was building. The four lice were closely examined to evaluate their sprightliness and vigor, odds were calculated, and bets were placed. Thonir watched with interest but declined to place his precious savings at risk.

The cook went to the galley and returned with four plates, which he set on the steps to the quarterdeck. Each louse was assigned a plate, on which it was carefully positioned, dead center, and held in place until all four were released at the count of three. Much shouting then ensued, as the crewmen cheered on their favorites, until the louse on the third plate (contributed by Gril) became the first to reach the edge. The race being won, the wagers were settled and all four contestants summarily squashed.

Vort, who had hazarded two *nemtek* on one of Thonir's lice, was disappointed but took his loss philosophically, while the cook, who had done well by acting as bookmaker, declined Thonir's hesitant offer of payment for the haircut. "Neermine, kit," he said. "Gladderdoot."

❦

Once they cast off, Thonir went aft to watch Karandoz retreat from view as they sailed across the bay and out into open water. Their destination lay almost directly to the south, but the wind was unfavorable, and the *Porpoise* had to tack in a southwest-southeast zigzag. The boatswain prevailed upon Vort and Thonir to do more chores until suppertime, at which point they consumed more dried fish, black bread, and Risdaric root vegetables, albeit with limited enthusiasm. The captain gave the cook permission, however, to appropriate one of the truckles of cheese for the galley, so everyone received a piece for dessert. Thonir had to admit that Vort was right about the Tseren prowess at cheese-making.

The *Porpoise* reached Trovan, capital of the Sovereign County of Risdar, about two hours before first light, so the captain waited until sunrise before taking the ship into the harbor and docking. After the size and vibrancy of Karandoz, Thonir was disappointed by what appeared to be little more than a sleepy fishing village, overlooked by a sturdy castle, but he was still eager to disembark and explore. This time there were no customs officials waiting on the wharf, and the captain let the crewmen go ashore almost immediately. Not all of them seemed particularly interested.

"I don' think we're unloadin' any cargo here," Vort said, as he and Thonir picked their way through the rutted, unpaved streets leading from the docks into town. "There ain't no market for pig iron in Risdar, and Uncle Vortan'll get a better price for the cheese in Hriss." They stopped to watch a nice-looking young woman go by carrying a basket of fish on her shoulder. "He'll prob'ly pick up s'more stuff, maybe some fleeces or some wool. The Risdar ain't up to much, really, beyond fishin' here on the coast and herdin' sheep up in the hills. So, we don' usually stop much longer'n it takes cook to buy more o' them purple roots of his."

Thonir was dimly aware that the Risdar had a reputation for exporting high quality wool. He did not know much more about them, except that the common folk spoke a language similar to Tseren.

The market square was paved with gray cobblestones, liberally coated with the dried mud tracked onto them when the surrounding unpaved streets were wet. The market itself was just getting started, but there were already large quantities of fish for sale, as well as freshly slaughtered lamb and mutton, a wide variety of vegetables, some local artisanal goods, and a very few imported manufactures. Thonir was debating whether to deplete his meager exchequer to buy a sort of savory crêpe cooked on the spot and served with ham and salted butter, when Vort elbowed him in the ribs and cried: "Ye gods, Fen! Get a loada *that!*"

Following Vort's quivering finger, Thonir's eyes widened as they alighted upon what was surely the most beautiful woman he had ever seen. Apparently in her mid-twenties, she was tall and slender, with dark hair and brilliant blue eyes, tempting pink lips, and the distinctive cheekbones Thonir had already noticed were characteristic of the Risdar. All of these features, taken together, lent an improbable glamour to her plain Risdaric peasant garb, as she arranged her goods for sale on the table of her market stall.

The two boys found themselves drawn ineluctably to her, like iron filings to a powerful magnet. Thonir hoped he did not look as moronic as Vort, who was practically drooling. Vexingly, communication proved difficult, as the young woman did not speak Ondiric, while Vort, with his limited command of Tseren, was unable to understand more than an occasional word or two of Risdaric, and those sometimes wrongly. Fortunately, the woman seemed amused rather than annoyed by these difficulties, giving Thonir time to notice that she emanated a strong magical potential. Assuming anyone had ever taught her to use magic, she would be a formidable practitioner. The thought hit him like a runaway oxcart: could she possibly be a wizard? He had never heard that there were wizards in Risdar, but no one had ever specifically told him there weren't any, either, and—the obvious linguistic barrier notwithstanding—the idea of apprenticing under this beauteous creature exceeded every fantasy his fertile adolescent brain had yet conceived. He looked at her earnestly and spoke the wizarding greeting, *"Kholenakht!"*

But alas, it was not to be. The woman turned and looked at him uncomprehendingly. Hitherto her attention had been focused on Vort and his faltering efforts to communicate, but now she seemed to notice Thonir for the first time, and her face took on a curious expression. Afterward, when his brain resumed normal functioning, he wondered if perhaps she, in turn, had sensed his own magical power, but at the time, as he met her intense azure gaze, rational thought deserted him in favor of borderline delirium.

Desperate to return this goddess's attention to himself, Vort made another foray into conversational Tseren. The woman turned to him and gave a baffled shrug. Then, speaking incomprehensibly in Risdaric, she attempted to redirect the boys' attention to the goods on her table, evidently hoping to convert this increasingly ridiculous encounter into a profitable one. Though Vort refused to be distracted, Thonir regained sufficient presence of mind to look where she was pointing. The table was piled high with little bundles of various kitchen-garden herbs, including parsley, chives, tarragon, and chervil, but Thonir immediately spotted something else, a stack of at least a dozen bundles of a magical herb he knew only by its wizarding name, *shigenkholan*. With greenish black leaves and bright red roots, it was, he knew, an essential ingredient in several useful potions, including—though Chodros had never taught him the recipe—one that imparted invisibility.

Although Thonir did not—could not—quite forget that he was in the presence of the most beautiful woman he had ever met (limited though his experience in this area had admittedly been), his normal thought processes somehow reasserted themselves. He picked up one of the bundles of *shigenkholan* and interrupted Vort, who was still in full flow, by asking "How much?" in Ondiric. To help convey his meaning, he pulled out his money purse and shook it, so that the coins jingled.

Nodding, the woman gave him a lovely smile that threatened to push his hormone-addled thoughts back into incoherence. She reached into her own purse, produced a Risdaric silver piece, and held up three fingers.

After an internal struggle, Thonir nodded and put down the bundle. "We'll be back," he promised in Ondiric, matching the words with some hand gestures he hoped would express the same idea. He grabbed his companion by the arm. "Come on, Vort. Let's go find the captain."

⚜

Vort was not pleased to be dragged away. "What's the matter with you, Fen? Didn' you *see* that gal? C'mon, *please* tell me you know a spell t'make her give it up!"

Thonir shook his head. "Don't be an idiot, Vort. That woman has enough magical power to drop us both dead in our tracks. I don't know if she knows how to use it, but I sure don't want to find out by trying something stupid." He looked urgently around the market, hoping to catch sight of Captain Vortan. "Now, help me look for your uncle."

Vort looked unhappily about. "There he is, over there, jawbonin' some wool merchant, looks like. Whaddaya wanna talk to *him* for?"

Thonir clucked his tongue impatiently. "Come on. You'll see." He crossed the square, followed by a grumbling Vort, and waited for a break in the men's conversation. "Have you got a moment, Captain?"

The captain nodded. "We're just about done here." He turned back to the wool merchant and gave him some final instructions. They shook hands. "All right, Fenith," he said, "what's up, and why does my nephew look like you've been feeding him earthworms?"

Thonir explained that he might have found a lucrative cargo. "*Shigenkholan* is pretty rare. The woman selling it"

(Vort groaned in despair) "was asking three of their silver pieces for a bundle with eight or ten full stalks. That may sound like a high price, but an alchemist in Mindor would charge at least that much for just one stalk."

The captain thought for a moment. "These are fresh herbs?" he asked. "Will they spoil if I can't find a buyer right away?"

Thonir shook his head. "No, they're just as potent dried. It looked like she had around twelve bundles, so maybe thirty-six of their silver pieces for something that will take up almost no space, weighs next to nothing, and should sell for eight or ten times as much."

"Retail," the captain pointed out. "I'd be lucky to get half that. But you're right, that's still a good return."

Thonir pointed out that the woman did not speak Ondiric, so the captain brought along his helmsman, who happened to be a Risdar, to act as interpreter. "One more thing, Captain," Thonir warned, as they crossed the market square. "This woman may be a sorceress—or even a witch!"

The helmsman grimaced. "Aye, thar be witches in Risdar, Cap'n, sure as devils spawn baby salamanders."

The captain cocked an eyebrow but did not seem too concerned. "Well then, our young wizard here will just have to keep an eye on her."

Vort groaned again.

⁂

The negotiation for the *shigenkholan* went smoothly, however, with no alarming magical interventions on either side. As it turned out, the woman had fourteen bundles of the herb, which brought the total price to forty-two Risdaric silver testoons, or two gold coronets, but she agreed to a bulk discount of four testoons. The captain had only one Risdaric coronet on him, but the woman accepted a Tseren gold *virin* in lieu of the other, returning four testoons in change and throwing in a twopenny bundle of tarragon for good measure. She also bestowed a grateful smile upon Thonir for facilitating the transaction, causing him to go slightly weak in the knees.

Their business complete, the captain thanked the woman, kissed her hand, and entrusted the pile of herbs to Thonir. "Come on, Vort," he said with a laugh. "Back to the ship. I can't have you standing around all day, eying this poor lass as though she were a raspberry *oraminta* drizzled with honey. Now scoot!"

11

Tenefir is a major seaport that has long played an important role in foreign trade. Straddling the River Tene, it has a picturesque medieval core, containing many quaint old houses.

— A Pocket Travel Guide to Hriss and Risdar

Back aboard the *Porpoise,* Thonir turned the tarragon over to the cook, who seemed pleased, and set about drying the *shigenkholan* to prevent it from spoiling. Chodros had often made him preserve herbs in this way, so he had no difficulty remembering the desiccation spell. Vort had retreated sullenly to his bunk directly upon arrival, so he missed his chance to see a little magic performed, but the cook seemed impressed by it, as best Thonir could tell from his peculiar commentary.

Although Risdaric customs inspectors had eventually taken up their posts on the wharf, they had shown no interest in the load of herbage Thonir carried aboard. When the captain's wool arrived later that afternoon, however, they bestirred themselves to count the bales and demand a trifling sum, which the captain paid without complaint after settling the wool merchant's much larger bill. Thonir then helped load the wool, using levitation to squeeze the bales into odd spaces below decks.

Conditions were favorable for casting off that evening, and before long the *Porpoise* rounded the tip of the Risdaric peninsula and began to follow the coast west-southwest to the Duchy of Hriss, arriving at the ducal city of Tenefir the next day, just in time to dock before dark.

Since they reached Tenefir too late to do business, the captain let the crew go ashore and amuse themselves. Thonir, having paid for the passage from Mindor, was not feeling very flush, but in the end he opted to go along anyway and drink the better part of a Mindoric penny's worth of beer to celebrate his arrival in Hriss. Here, he hoped, his fortunes would turn, and he would find a wizard to take him on.

It was an enjoyable evening. The Hrissic beer was a signal improvement over the Tseren ale, and there was a good deal of joking and laughing. Vort had recovered his good humor and told some particularly ridiculous stories that kept everyone amused. But the main thing from Thonir's point of view was that the crew of the *Porpoise* had accepted him as a worthy companion. He had also come to like them in turn. It was a pleasant, unaccustomed feeling to be among friends—albeit a feeling tinged with melancholy at the thought that he was soon to part ways with them.

The next morning the captain went into town to make arrangements and did not return with wagons until mid-morning. Thonir then did what he could to help shift the iron, cheese, and wool, but he exhausted his *silendras* long before the job was done. He then helped transfer the heavy truckles of cheese to one of the wagons by hand.

Once the captain had finished paying the stiff duty the Hrissic customs officer assessed on the cheese, he excused

Thonir from accompanying the wagons to the warehouse. "You've done enough, Fenith," he said. "You're a good lad, and I hope you find a good master to finish your training." He produced two stalks of dried *shigenkholan* from his pocket. "I want to thank you for pointing me to this herb," he said. "I visited an alchemist this morning and sold him eight stalks for about five times what I paid for them." He handed the two stalks to Thonir. "I think you deserve these as a finder's fee."

Thonir's normally serious face broke into a smile. He placed the dried stalks carefully in his bag, which he had retrieved earlier along with his blanket in preparation for departure. He thanked the captain and said his goodbyes to the rest of the crew. Vort gave him a playful punch to the arm and expressed the hope that they would meet again after Thonir had risen to the rank of court magician somewhere, no doubt giving him his pick of high-born beauties. Thonir expressed due skepticism regarding the likelihood of this scenario. "You take care of yourself, Vort," he said. "And keep an eye out for Gril's sea monsters!"

A city comparable in size to Mindor and Karandoz, Tenefir was filled with narrow, twisting streets, laid out without plan or design. Its southerly location meant that it was warmer than cities further north, and Thonir sensed that spring was further along. If he ended up having to sleep rough, he told himself, it would not be so bad—well, not *quite* so bad.

He entered a neighborhood filled with the shops of artisans. He looked around, hoping to find someone who would be likely to know something about the city's magicians. Before long, he came across a goldsmith's. Thinking the proprietor would be likely to have had dealings with a magician for security work, he went inside. A large, round woman of middle years loomed behind the counter, glaring at a muscular young man who was sitting in the corner, glaring back at her. Thonir suspected a family squabble. He could hear the sound of delicate hammering from the room behind, where the actual goldsmithing was happening.

"Excuse me," he began, "can you tell me if there are any wizards in Tenefir?"

The woman redirected her glare toward him. He could almost feel the heat of her angry gaze. "Ain't no wizards in this shop," she growled. "We sell the finest luxury goods here, crafted from the purest gold. Nothin' you can afford, from the looks of you." She gestured at him as though she were shooing away a stray dog. "Off with you. Go on, then, boy, git!"

The muscular young man stood up and clenched his fists, looking suddenly hopeful at the prospect of violence. "You want I should thump him, Ma?"

Thonir made a placatory gesture with his free hand. "No need for that!" he said, backing up hastily. "I'm going."

Disappointed, the muscular young man sank back into his seat. "Aw, crap," he said. "Stupid punk kid, lookin' fer wizards in a goldsmithy."

Back on the street, Thonir marveled at his luck in so often encountering such unpleasant people. He shook his head, realizing that he was already missing the friendly crew of the *Porpoise*. He continued to explore the city regardless, hoping to stumble upon the premises of a freelance wizard. After a time, however, he came upon a shop advertised by a sign emblazoned with alchemical symbols. Inside the small, cramped establishment was a youngish man with chemical burns on his hands, fiddling with an alembic over a small, apparently magical flame. Seeing a potential customer, this person extinguished the flame and asked how he might be of service.

Thonir decided to try a different tack than he had employed at the goldsmith's. "Do you have the magic herb that wizards call *shigenkholan?*" he asked. "I don't know the Gantelic name."

"*Mingalia,*" returned the alchemist mildly. "What a coincidence! I just took some in stock this morning." He produced a glass jar containing the eight stalks from under the counter. "Four silver griffins a stalk. Expensive, I know, but useful stuff. Versatile!"

Thonir feigned a crestfallen look. "Too expensive for me, I'm afraid. Say, what can you tell me about any wizards here in Tenefir, who might be in need of an advanced apprentice? Does the Hrissic court magician happen to be a wizard?"

The alchemist eyed him appraisingly. "No, I'm afraid not. His grace employs a sorcerer. There *is* a freelance wizard named Trofim, who lives just a few minutes from here. His practice is quite well established, but I've never heard that he was looking for an apprentice. Still, you might give him a try. The only other magician in town is a young sorceress, though I gather she actually knows a fair amount of wizardry, too. A clever girl, but struggling, I think, to find clients. I can't imagine she'd be of any use to you."

Thonir shook his head. "No, it doesn't sound like it." He asked for directions to find the wizard Trofim. "What's he like, anyway?"

The alchemist paused, apparently debating how indiscreet to be about one of his primary customers. "Oh, he's friendly enough. Bit of a glad-hander, really. His father's big in the Tenefir Merchant Guild, so he's got good connections and knows how to use them." He gave Thonir directions on how to get to the man's house. "He's got a sign over the door. A lightning bolt. You can't miss it."

Thonir thanked him, expressed regret at not being able to afford the *shigenkholan,* and took his leave.

A tiny old woman answered his knock. She was dressed as a servant in a long shapeless gray kirtle and carried a worn-out broom. Her wispy white hair and cataracts reminded Thonir of the Inirochian woman he had seen at the slave mart in Karandoz. When she spoke, however, her voice belied any impression of pathos. "Whaddaya want?" she demanded belligerently.

Thonir—who was now forcefully reminded of Chodros instead—hung his head and shuffled his feet, as though detected in some infraction. "I . . . I wish to speak with the wizard Trofim," he mumbled.

"Speak up, boy!"

"I want to speak with Trofim," he said loudly.

The old woman shook her broom at him. "But does he wanna speak with you?" She glared. "Aye, there's the rub."

Thonir looked at her pleadingly. "Perhaps you could ask him?"

She considered this novel concept for a moment. "You wait," she said and slammed the door in his face.

Perplexed, Thonir did just that, for several anxious minutes, until a smiling man of about thirty reopened the door. He was wearing slippers with curled toes, along with a midnight-blue cloak embroidered with golden stars and moons and mystical symbols, almost as though he were costumed as a wizard for a stage play.

"Good day, young man," he said, looking Thonir over. Evidently the boy's spare clothes and new haircut passed muster. "You wish to consult with me?"

Thonir nodded. "Yes, please."

"Then, come in, come in," the wizard urged. "Don't mind Maga," he added apologetically, as he led Thonir into his receiving room—which was dressed like a theatrical set, with mystical symbols on the walls, stars on the ceiling, and a pentangle in one corner of the floor. "She doesn't usually answer the door, but the lovely Petrilla is feeling unwell today." He sat down at a small table on which stood a crystal ball and a smoldering stick of incense. "Now then, my boy, what can I do for you?"

Telling the precise truth did not seem advisable, so Thonir chose his words cautiously. He had been practicing this speech for some time. "My name is Fenith, and I was in my sixth year as apprentice to the wizard Chilteros in Vildenon, when he was killed last month in a terrible fire that also destroyed all my spell books and study materials. I have therefore come south in search of a new master, under whose guidance I might study and finish my apprenticeship. I heard you well spoken of, and it is my hope that you would consider taking me on—or, if you aren't in a position to do so, that you know of some other wizard of skill and wisdom, to whom I might apply."

Trofim rubbed his ear. "I see. What a sad misfortune to have befallen you." He stroked his chin. "I've never considered taking an apprentice, but I suppose it would have certain advantages. No doubt it would please Petrilla if someone took over some of her less pleasant duties." Something in his tone suggested that keeping the lovely Petrilla well content with her employment was a priority. "Still—and forgive me for mentioning it—I do not sense any significant aura of magical power about you. Not much point in an apprentice without *silendras,* is there."

Thonir scuffed his toe on the thick imported rug. "I *am* tapped out right now," he admitted, "but that's because I spent the morning levitating a heavy cargo of pig iron out of the hold of a merchant ship."

"That does sound taxing," Trofim conceded. "Makes me tired just thinking about it!" He rubbed his ear again. "I don't know, kid. I'm not sure I would have a great deal to teach you. Most of the work here is pretty mundane stuff—security commissions, a little bogus divination, the occasional love potion—magicks you've probably already covered by now." He shook his head. "No, I'm sorry, but I really think you'd be better off with someone else. You might try Elantrovir in Ksetilan. He's a man of deep experience, with a strong interest in the more esoteric aspects of our art. You could learn a lot from him. Or there's an Esdiric wizard named Khish practicing in the Grand Duchy of Modir. I've heard good things about his abilities—at least I seem to remember doing so."

Someone else might have tried to convince the wizard to change his mind, but Thonir felt too dispirited to argue. He scratched unhappily at a flea. "Well, thank you for the recommendations," he said politely. He scratched again, prompting a thought. "Say, I wonder if you can help me with a different matter. Among the spells I lost was one eradicating bloodsucking vermin. On my journey here, I seem to have picked up some unwelcome guests. How much would you charge to cast a spell to rid me of them?"

Trofim looked vaguely alarmed to hear that Thonir had brought bloodsucking vermin into the house. "Well, um, I suppose I could do it for one copper dragonet."

"I'm afraid I don't have any Hrissic money," Thonir said, taking out his purse. "Would you take a Tseren copper *tüzen?*"

Trofim weighed the proffered coin in his hand. "Well, this is quite a bit lighter than a dragonet, but yes, I suppose I could accept it out of—shall we say—professional courtesy." He retrieved a heavy grimoire from a stack of books piled carelessly next to the wall. "Not a spell I happen to have memorized, but let's see . . . vermin . . . bloodsucking . . . eradication of—yes, here we are." He studied the spell for a moment. "Hmm, yes, quite straightforward." He recited the short incantation in the wizarding tongue and gestured at Thonir. "That should do it."

Thonir could not immediately be sure the spell had worked (though it had), but he repeated the incantation to himself several times, determined to commit it to memory. "Thank you." He hesitated for a moment. "I suspect that the passage to Ksetilan will cost more than I have. When the fire happened, I was at the alchemist's, purchasing *shigen-kholan* for my master, or *mingalia* as they call it in Gantelic." He produced the two stalks from his bag. "Would you perhaps be interested in acquiring these? I paid eight pieces of imperial silver for the pair of them in Vildenon, so perhaps eight of your Hrissic silver griffins would be fair?"

Trofim examined the dried herbs with interest. "It is a useful ingredient," he admitted, "but eight silver griffins seems high. I would be willing to pay six."

The boy nodded. "Done!"

This important transaction completed, Thonir hastened back to the docks, hoping to find a ship to carry him to Ksetilan, which lay further to the south. He was, of course, disappointed not to have secured an apprenticeship in Tenefir, but Trofim had not impressed him as a great and powerful wizard, so no doubt the man was right that he would do better to find a new master elsewhere. Furthermore, he now had six silver griffins to finance the search. It was more money than he had ever possessed in his life, and it gave him a pleasant—though illusory—sense of security.

12

Ksetilan is an exciting destination, with a pleasant climate, fine beaches, and many gastronomic delights—though be warned that visits to the casino are likely to bust the budget traveler's travel budget!

— Hriss on 10 Crowns a Day

Thonir had to approach the captains of no fewer than six ships before he found one headed to Ksetilan who was willing to take him on—and did not also frighten the life out of him. Indeed, the captain of the second ship seemed so villainous, as did the ship's mate, that Thonir felt certain they would rob him of everything he owned and throw him overboard as soon as they reached the open ocean.

The captain of the sixth ship—a large cog called the *Cormorant*—might not have been as amiable as his counterpart on the *Porpoise,* but he made a favorable impression of intelligence and efficiency. This time, Thonir did not propose working in exchange for a lower fare. The ship was already loaded, and he had learned from his experience in Tenefir that he would do better not to exhaust his *silendras* helping to unload it upon arrival. He agreed instead to pay one silver griffin.

So long as there was no unfavorable change in the weather, the plan was for the ship to sail the next morning, when the tide went out. Thonir was welcome to spend the night on board, but his fare did not include meals, so he went back into town to buy provisions, spending some of his remaining copper and tin coins on a boule of rye bread, a block of Hrissic cheese, and four freshly harvested carrots. (The merchants in Tenefir, he found, turned up their noses at the rusty iron *nemtek*.)

The *Cormorant* was a Hrissic ship, based in Tenefir, and its crew was a mix of Ondir and Esdir. The weather did in fact remain favorable the next morning, and the ship cast off at first light, with a hold full of rock salt from the mines in the Saalic Mountains to the north. As they sailed down the Hrissic coast, Thonir passed the time conversing with members of the crew, especially the Esdir, taking advantage of the opportunity to practice his Esdiric and learn its nautical terms, a vocabulary set Chodros had rarely employed. Vocabulary was in fact Thonir's weak spot, for he had a passable grasp of Esdiric grammar, and his accent was rather good.

As the sun was setting, however, the crewman in the crow's nest raised the alarm, and Thonir saw that some huge and fearsome thing had surfaced a hundred yards to port. Gril had been right: there *were* monstrous strange creatures in the southern waters. This one was serpent-like, with a great, scaly head and a long, segmented, blue-green body that was at least three times as long as the ship. Before Thonir could get more than a quick impression, however, the aquatic menace submerged again, though its sinuous locomotion remained discernible just below the surface, as the creature headed straight for the *Cormorant*.

Cursing by all the demons in hell—and a few more besides—the captain ordered a change in course of two points to starboard, so as to take better advantage of the wind, while also bringing the vessel closer to shore, where perhaps this leviathan might hesitate to follow. Nevertheless, the serpent quickly closed the distance separating them. It rose up out of the water with an eerie screech, its thick wet scales and cold ophidian eyes glistening in the failing sunlight. Several members of the crew screamed in terror, as the monster snatched a hapless sailor from the main deck with astonishing speed, seizing the entire upper half of his body in its powerful jaws. There was a horrific effusion of blood. Crewmen dashed frantically about the deck, desperate to avoid becoming the next victim. Only the ship's mate had to courage to try to gaff the beast with a boat hook, though without success.

Cowering amidships behind a barrel of drinking water, Thonir struggled to tamp down his surging panic and decide what to do. If only the creature had resurfaced at some distance from the ship, a well-placed fireball might have deterred it, but at such close range the only thing he could think of was his befuddling spell—which had worked on the brewery's wolfhound back in Mindor, after all. As the monster lifted its chosen dinner—or rather, its intended appetizer—high into the air, Thonir took a deep breath and cast the spell with all the *silendras* he could muster. For a tense moment, nothing seemed to have happened, but then the giant serpent began to sway drunkenly, dropped its now lifeless prey into the sea, and slid back down beneath the waves in a state of utter stupefaction.

⚜

Thonir had no success persuading the captain that wizardry had thwarted the monster's attack rather than luck or providence. In the confusion, no one had seen him gesticulate at the creature, and with his *silendras* exhausted he was unable to demonstrate the befuddling spell on a member of the crew. He would have appreciated at least a partial reimbursement of his fare in recognition of his valuable service, but none was forthcoming.

The *Cormorant* reached its destination the next morning, a good two hours after daybreak. Thonir could see that Ksetilan was a city of fair size, with solid fortifications and a busy harbor. He disembarked with his belongings as soon as the ship had docked, and headed for the city center. While he felt nervous about interrupting two city watchmen, whom he saw chatting with a pretty, dark-haired girl selling eggs and butter on the main market square, he reasoned that they were as likely as anyone to know the whereabouts of the city's magicians, and more likely than some.

"Elantrovir?" asked the first watchman irritably, while his colleague exploited the distraction to reach for the girl's waist. "Never heard of him."

The dairymaid slapped the second watchman's hand away. "I have," she said. "My mother tol' me never trust a wizard—*nor yet a watchman!*—but this feller, he's old as dirt and never gives me no trouble." She slapped the watchman's hand away again. "Not like these two clowns."

The second watchman feigned offense. "She called us clowns, Ghinth," he protested. "Us honest protectators of law'n'order in this dangerous metropolitis."

"Ungrateful wench," opined the first watchman, shaking his head sadly. "No respect fer authority, Mitt, that's the problem wit' young folk t'day."

"Too true, Ghinth, too true," lamented the second watchman. He extracted a straw from the tidy display of fresh eggs and began to use it as a toothpick.

The girl ignored them both. "He's a strange ole coot," she told Thonir. "I s'pose that comes with bein' a wizard and all, but the man likes his dairy goods, he does, an' he pays for 'em without bellyachin' about the price—*or tryin' to cop a feel, neither!*" She glared at the second watchman, who grinned back unashamedly.

Thonir gave her a sympathetic look that he hoped conveyed a measure of apology for being of the same gender as these two louts. "Where can I find him then, miss?"

She gave him half a smile. "He's got a fine big house in the rich part of town." She pointed across the square. "You follow that street yonder all the way up to the end, and you'll find it, sure nuff. Just look for the big dragon-thing over the door."

Thonir thanked her and said goodbye. He felt sorry to leave the two watchmen in possession, but he suspected she was a match for them, and indeed no sooner had he stepped away from the market stall than he heard her exclaim: "Now, then, off with you two loafers! You'll scare my customers away. I won't have it!"

Should Elantrovir take him on, Thonir decided, he would be more than happy to assume responsibility for the wizard's dairy shopping.

✤

The indicated street was long and winding, but it grew wider, straighter, and cleaner, as it led into a wealthy residential neighborhood filled with large townhouses built of sandstone and fancy cream-colored brick. Tall trees (some of which struck Thonir, who had never seen palms before, as very strange indeed) overtopped the walls of private pleasure gardens. The stench of human waste, noticeable elsewhere if you were not used to it, faded here to a barely perceptible bouquet mingled with the wholesome scent of spring vegetation. Thonir tried to look as though he belonged in such exalted surroundings, as he strode up the street under the suspicious eye of city watchmen, who were much more plentiful here than in neighborhoods where crime was common.

At the end of the street stood a grand mansion. Embedded in the wall over the front door, and stretching some twelve feet in length, was a series of brightly painted ceramic tiles, depicting a great winged reptile—the dairymaid's "dragon-thing"—which Thonir recognized from Ondiric folktales as a wyrm. For several minutes he gazed at it in wonder. Then, screwing up his courage, he ascended the steps to the door, seized the brass doorknocker (itself in the shape of a wyrm), and brought it firmly down three times in succession.

He waited quite some time, and was just reaching for the knocker again, when he heard the sound of a heavy bolt sliding. He retreated back down the steps to avoid being hit by the massive oak door, as it swung slowly open. In the doorway stood an old man with long white hair, a bushy white beard, and thick white eyebrows. His face was pale and wrinkled, but his eyes were bright. He was wearing sandals and drab gray robes, and in one arthritic hand he held a brass ear trumpet. He contemplated Thonir without speaking.

Thonir hesitated, unsure whether he was actually in the presence of the magician himself, or one of his servants. "I seek the wizard Elantrovir," he said at last, rather loudly.

The old man nodded. "And you have found him." He positioned the ear trumpet in case his visitor had anything to add.

Thonir recited much the same introductory speech he had given in Trofim's receiving room two days earlier.

Elantrovir listened. When Thonir was finished, he pointed a crooked finger at the boy. On it was a silver ring set with onyx. "You have told me an alarming number of lies," he said gravely, "starting with your name and that of your former master. Yet the substance of your story is true. You interest me strangely, young man. I wish to know the reason for these falsehoods." He gave a grim, crooked smile. "So, come in. But first," he said, pointing upward, "tell me what is written above the door."

Thonir saw that there was an inscription in the wizarding tongue he had not noticed before. *"Rishgid shontaiin,"* he read. "The Wyrm's Lair."

Elantrovir nodded approvingly. "Just so. Whatever his true name, I perceive that your former master was indeed an Esdir, for he taught you to speak the mystic tongue with his own native accent." He stepped back to make way for the boy to enter. "It is of no consequence. Now, come in, young man, and explain yourself."

The wizard led Thonir down a wide entry hall that was dimly lit by magic. "Most people today believe the wyrm to be mythical," he remarked, "but it is only extinct. The last one died over five hundred years ago, during the Time of Troubles." He sighed. "No doubt that is for the best, as they were very destructive creatures, but it does seem a pity." He opened the doors at the end of the passage with the merest wave of his hand. The room beyond was filled with esoteric objects, including a number of small, intricate machines, whose purpose Thonir could scarcely guess, as well as more books than he had ever seen in one place before. Elantrovir cleared a stack of parchments from a chair with another wave of his hand and invited the boy to sit. "I do not entertain many guests," he noted, "but perhaps you will join me in a cup of *noriboth*." Without waiting for a reply, he clapped his hands and the herbal infusion began to prepare itself over a magical fire. "As you can see, I keep no servants. They annoyed me, so gradually I let them all go. Instead I have enchanted the house to clean itself and tend to my needs, such as they are. It is also many years since I last employed an apprentice. Having made my fortune, I am long since retired from commercial wizardry, in favor of my own private esoteric studies, so I have had little need of one." The *noriboth* poured itself into two small cups. The wizard took one himself, while the other winged its way over to Thonir. "It is quite hot," the old man warned. "Take care not to scald your tongue." He took a seat not far from the boy's chair and readied his ear trumpet. "Now then, tell me the true details of your story. There is, incidentally, no need to shout. This instrument is so highly enchanted that I can hear the mice conversing within the walls—though admittedly I cannot understand what they are saying."

This remark sidetracked Thonir's thoughts for a moment. "You have not cast a spell to eradicate them?" he asked, surprised.

The wizard shook his head. "Rats, yes, but I have no quarrel with mice. Now speak."

Reluctantly, Thonir rehearsed his unhappy story, leaving out certain specifics he found embarrassing or shameful but taking care not to say anything false. Occasionally, Elantrovir interrupted with incisive questions, and once he reminded Thonir not to let his *noriboth* grow cold, but otherwise he listened without comment. When Thonir finished, the wizard questioned him closely about the spells Chodros had taught him, placing the boy in a bit of a bind when it came to mentioning the ones he had taught himself without Chodros's permission. In the end, he admitted to having stolen them, hoping that Elantrovir would give greater weight to his determination to learn than to his willingness to deceive his former master.

The wizard gave him another grim smile. "I knew Chodros when he was a young man," he said, "and I can believe he was a difficult master." He paused before adding, half to himself, "As no doubt was I." Setting down his cup of *noriboth,* he got up and strode around the room with greater vigor than Thonir would have expected for a man of his obvious antiquity. "And as I have told you, I no longer have need of an apprentice. If I were to take one now, it would be solely to train someone so brilliant that having done so would burnish my own legacy." He paused again before admitting, "Yes, I have grown that selfish in my old age." He looked at Thonir directly. "I sense that you are a young man of talent, but not of genius. Your *silendras* is strong, but not exceptional. You have learned—indeed, in some cases taught yourself—spells that require considerable intelligence, but I am doubtful that yours is the vanishingly rare mind that can apprehend the deepest mysteries of our art." He looked away, somewhat guiltily, before letting the axe fall. "I am sorry, young man, but I will not take you as my apprentice."

Thonir said nothing. He looked crestfallen, this time for the simple reason that he was—very much so.

Elantrovir resumed his peregrinations around the room. "I am mindful that you have journeyed far to see me," he said, "and I regret having disappointed you. Perhaps if I were to teach you a useful spell before you left, you would not feel your effort was entirely in vain."

Thonir swallowed hard. "I . . . I would appreciate that, yes, Eminence," he said humbly.

"Chodros appears to have taught you what any wizard might require to make a tedious career in commercial security work," Elantrovir noted, "but I fear he failed to equip you sufficiently to face the dangers of the wider world into which you have now stumbled. I do not know you well enough to feel comfortable teaching you an offensive spell you might misuse to hurt others, but every wizard should have some good defensive spells in his repertoire." He walked over to a standing desk, selected a quill and a small sheet of parchment, and began to write, while simultaneously explaining aloud: "The 'Magician's Shield' throws up an invisible barrier that is impervious to most physical attacks, though its size and strength are of course dependent on the amount of *silendras* you choose to expend. Even a rather feeble casting will block an ordinary sword or arrow, but it takes a slightly stronger one to block a magical weapon." He put down the quill. "With regard to hostile spells, an adequately powered shield will block a physical attack—such as a fireball or a lightning bolt—but no matter how much power you commit, the shield will not block subtler spells, such as those to induce sleep or fear." He handed over the parchment, now covered in wizarding script written in a careful hand that gave no hint of his age or arthritis. "It is not an easy spell to master," he continued. "As you can see, it involves no incantation, for in a dangerous situation you may not have time for one. Instead, you must conjure the shield purely by the power of your mind. At first, you may find that hand gestures help you define its size and shape, but that is an aid you should soon set aside, as it will only slow you down, while betraying useful information to your opponent."

Thonir studied the spell with growing excitement, trying to grasp its complex instructions on how to access and apply his *silendras*.

Elantrovir gave him a moment to take it in. "Now then, cast a small, weak shield between us. Concentrate. Focus. Picture the invisible shield in your mind as though it were a tangible object. Draw upon your *silendras* according to the strictures of the spell, and prevent me from poking you in the chest."

Thonir sustained several embarrassing pokes, but he persevered, fumbling his way toward the correct technique, until the wizard's finger crumpled in midair.

"Ouch," said Elantrovir, giving the ill-used digit a shake. "Yes, my boy, you seem to have wrapped your mind around the concept."

It was a cruel irony, Thonir later felt, that on the very day he learned a powerful new defensive spell, he should be set upon by robbers and beaten senseless. After leaving the Wyrm's Lair, he returned to the docks and found a ship to take him to the Grand Duchy of Modir, further along the Hrissic coast. With several hours to spare before the captain expected to set sail, he decided to spend the time exploring Ksetilan. Having ill-advisedly wandered into a part of town the city watch left largely to its own devices, he found himself suddenly seized under the armpits by two passing thugs, who slammed him against the wall of an adjacent tumble-down building. The first thug then punched him in the gut, while the second grabbed his head and slammed it repeatedly against the wall, until everything went black.

When he regained consciousness, Thonir was sprawled on a pile of rubble inside the abandoned building, his clothing askew and his head throbbing. It took a moment for his vision to come into focus, at which point he saw that the roof was mostly gone. Daylight was beginning to fade, and his ship would have sailed by now. His coin purse was gone, along with his blanket, and the old sack containing nearly all of his possessions. As the absolute wretchedness of his situation sank in, the boy curled up into a ball amidst the rubble and—for the first time since the death of his parents four years earlier—broke down and wept.

13

Parchment—a writing material prepared from the skins of sheep, goats, and calves—was for centuries the primary means of preserving the written word. Given the elaborate processes involved in its manufacture, which included washing, liming, unhairing, and scraping the skins, which were then washed again and stretched on frames, dusted with chalk, and rubbed with pumice, parchment was an expensive product—a circumstance that greatly impeded the dissemination of knowledge prior to the importation of paper-making technology from the West near the end of the medieval period.

— *The Encyclopædia Ondiricana* (12th ed.)

Thonir woke early, as first light penetrated the wide gaps in the roof. He stretched, cautiously exploring his body's many discomforts. The rubble had provided a poor mattress, and he now ached in places the robbers had not struck him. Still, spring nights were balmy in this, the southernmost tip of Ondiran, so at least he had not suffered from the cold. Indeed, had the robbers not stolen his blanket, he would have placed it under rather than over himself. The beating had robbed him of all his remaining *silendras,* but he could feel that the night's sleep had restored some of it, and he would be capable of casting a few spells, if need be, despite the goose egg on the back of his head and the throbbing behind his eyes.

Getting up, rather unsteadily, he took inventory of what the robbers had left him, namely his clothes (now torn in

101

places) and his belt (with its concealed picklocks) but not his shoes (worn though they had been). In his pockets, he found the piece of hardtack the ship's mate had given him aboard the *Porpoise* and a length of string he had picked up along the way. Surveying the rubble, he found that the robbers, in going through his things, had discarded Elantrovir's parchment and Chodros's self-inking quill as worthless. He also found two of the eight iron *nemtek* that had been in his purse, similarly cast aside. A little excavation turned up three more, while the rest remained lost for the potential benefit of future archaeologists.

Having eaten nothing since breakfast the previous day, Thonir was hungry. He therefore broke the hardtack forcibly into smaller pieces and placed one of them in his mouth, hoping it would eventually soften enough for him to chew. As he gradually consumed this unsatisfying meal, he pondered his predicament.

He was altogether too ashamed to consider returning to Elantrovir for help, and he now had no money for passage to Modir. Five *nemtek* were worth less than a Mindoric half-penny—and then seemingly only in Tserenets. While he could try to use magic to induce a ship's captain to take him along for nothing, the dishonesty of the scheme troubled his increasingly sensitive conscience. He would, in any case, still be penniless upon arrival, unless he also used magic to start stealing outright, thus sinking back into the moral quagmire from which he thought he had escaped when he left Mindor.

He was contemplating Elantrovir's parchment, idly running his fingers over its smooth, carefully treated surface, when an alternative occurred to him. He did not like it—indeed, he found the idea most uncongenial—but it was practical, it involved wizardry, and it was honest. He put the parchment in his pocket, along with the quill, the string, and the five *nemtek,* while the last piece of hardtack he put in his mouth. He looked carefully through the open doorway and stepped out into the street.

As he traversed the cobblestones back into a more salubrious part of town, Thonir had reason to regret that the robbers had taken his shoes. Before long, he approached a pair of city watchmen. "Excuse me, sergeant," he said, having spotted the badge of rank on the older of the two men, "where will I find the tanneries here in Ksetilan?"

"Just follow yer nose," the sergeant replied, laughing, "and ya can't miss 'em!"

The younger watchman grinned but condescended to provide a more helpful answer. "Outside Black Tower Gate," he explained, pointing back in the direction from which Thonir had come. "Just as far away from rich folk, as the city elders could put 'em."

Thonir thanked him and retraced his steps. He had no difficulty finding the aptly named Black Tower Gate, which loomed over the poorest section of the city like a giant predator, and well before he reached it, the stench of his ultimate destination had reached him. Passing through the gate, he entered the realm of the odoriferous trades—a space of exile beyond the city walls where the tanners, dyers, chandlers, and knackermen earned their livings. Singling out what appeared to be the largest of the tanneries, he approached two workers who were pulling hides from a large vat of urine so they could begin to scrape the hair from them.

"Morning," he said. "Where can I find your boss?"

One of the workers jerked his finger in the direction of a hut located deeper in the yard.

"Thanks," said Thonir. He straightened his shoulders and headed that way, wishing all the more fervently that he still had his shoes. Had the robbers somehow contrived to steal his sense of smell instead, he would have been much happier. Outside the hut, an old woman was softening a hide by pounding it with dung, while two young men were poking at the contents of a lime pit with long paddles. Additional pits of noxious chemicals, containing hides in various stages of the tanning process, lay temporarily unattended.

"Good morning," Thonir said to the middle-aged man inside the hut, who was trimming finished pieces of fine leather with a sharp knife.

Bent over his workbench, the tanner nodded in reply. He was short and heavy-set, with close-cropped red hair and several days' growth of reddish beard.

"Tell me," Thonir continued, "do you produce parchment here, or just tanned goods?"

The tanner straightened up. "Aye, far'n'away the best parchment in Ksetilan."

Thonir tapped himself on the chest, hoping to appear more confident than he felt. "I can help you make it even better," he asserted. "And quicker, too!"

"No kiddin'," said the tanner, putting down his knife. "And how 'xactly you gonna do that, young pup like you?"

"Magic," replied Thonir. "I'm an apprentice wizard—or at least I was before my poor master passed." Having noticed a Cantiferian holy symbol on the wall, he added a parenthetical, "The saints and prophets bless his soul!" He looked the tanner in the eye. "If there's one thing an apprentice magician learns how to do, it's work with parchment." This claim was true enough. Chodros had always needed more parchment (much of it, admittedly, for his apprentice's own notes), and Thonir thus spent endless hours at the tanneries downwind of Mindor, casting the spells Chodros had taught him to speed each step of the slow process of producing the stuff, while also yielding a higher quality output from lower quality hides, so as to save his master money. Even more important to Chodros were spells to produce the smoothest possible writing surface, over which a quill could glide effortlessly, and to make the parchment lie flat, regardless of the changes in humidity that made unenchanted sheets buckle. Thonir had hated the whole foul business, even though it did enable him to secretly appropriate small scraps of parchment for himself.

The tanner pursed his lips thoughtfully, as Thonir explained the spells he knew and the advantages they would bring. "Well," he said, when the boy finished, "'Tain't no skin off my nose t'give you a shot. What yer promisin' ain't nothin' to sneeze at—if you kin deliver. I mean, I ain't countin' my chickens, but waste not, want not, I always say, an' a ferret saved is a ferret earned" (the Hrissic brass ferret being worth roughly the same as the Mindoric copper penny).

Negotiations followed, during which the tanner's wife ("the little woman") wandered in and was consulted regarding the practicalities of providing Thonir with room and board. Even shorter than her husband and compactly built, she had a wide but pleasant face and took an immediate maternal interest in the boy. "He kin sleep in the shed behind the chicken coop," she decided. "You'll be right comfy in there," she assured Thonir, "leastwise now the weather's warm. The cockerel crows sometimes durin' the night, but you'll soon get used to him."

Ultimately, they agreed to a one-week trial period, during which Thonir would show what he could do, sleep in the shed, tolerate the cockerel, and partake of meals with the family. If, at the end of that time, the tanner wished to hire him, they would return to the question of cash wages, having perhaps established what Thonir's help was actually worth—for the proof, the tanner asserted, was in the puddin'.

Thonir, who had always understood the proof of the pudding to be in the eating, nodded and said nothing.

14

Odoriferous trades and other necessary nuisances shall not be licensed within the city walls.

— Ksetilan city statute from the reign
of Duke Hrontilar I, Year Six

Thonir's first week at the tannery passed slowly. He had to perform a great deal of uninteresting, repetitive, and taxing magic. The tanner, Voldin, continued to display a remarkable ability to express himself almost solely by means of cliché, while his wife, Gorta, showed a determination to see her new charge put on weight, which would have been more tolerable had she been a better cook. There were three adult sons, all of them large and lumbering—to Thonir's surprise, for he would have expected such toxic surroundings to have produced a clan of stunted gnomes. They worked hard but rarely said a word, especially to him. Indeed, by the end of the week Thonir began to wonder if the youngest son was even capable of speech. The tannery's other workers clearly had not been hired for their conversational skills, either. Indeed, had they possessed any skills whatever, they would surely have found work elsewhere.

The shed was tolerable, apart from its pervasive odor of chicken droppings, which mingled aggressively with the background stench of the tannery. The cockerel did in fact crow quite often during the night, but whether to frighten off rats and skunks and other nocturnal predators, or because he was having heroic dreams about doing so, Thonir could not determine. Thonir himself dreamt once about the pretty dairymaid at the market, but otherwise only about enchanting vast vats of piss and mountains of dog shit, so as to make them even nastier than nature intended, all for the greater glory of his employer.

Gorta did repair the incidental damage the robbers had done to Thonir's clothes, for which he was duly grateful, and she loaned him a pair of wooden clogs, which were uncomfortable but at least protected his feet from the foulness of the yard. Voldin expressed astonishment that Thonir's spells were so effective, remarking repeatedly that they were better than a kick in the teeth. He also said they showed that there was more than one way to skin a cat, something he presumably already knew from personal experience. At the end of the trial period, he offered Thonir one copper dragonet a week (the Cantiferian week being seven days). By this time, Thonir had learned enough about Hrissic currency to know that there were five copper dragonets in a silver griffin, and he had worked out that one of the heavy coins was worth about two Mindoric copper pennies. It was a solid wage, but he knew he was adding considerable value to the tanner's business, especially since many of his spells were useful for tanning leather as well as for making parchment. He therefore tried to hold out for more, but Voldin maintained that tanners were not made of money and beggars could not be choosers.

❧

The coming weeks were difficult. Boredom competed with depression and self-loathing for mastery of Thonir's psyche. Summer weather came early to Ksetilan, and the heat only made things worse. The smells and flies native to the tannery were bad enough, but when the knackerman next door suffered a minor accident and fell behind in his work, the carcasses piled up in his yard and began to rot. Thonir cursed himself for having failed to memorize an air-freshening spell Chodros had taught him, not that he would have had enough *silendras* to spare for it to have made much of an impact. Voldin kept him working, apart from the Cantiferian Day of Rest at the end of each week, when the boy accompanied the family to a temple of their faith just inside Black Tower Gate and prayed in desperation for a release from this purgatory. After services, he would usually wander aimlessly around the city. When he happened to see a girl his own age, however, he was too ashamed of the stench that clung to his clothes to approach her. On occasion he would practice the defensive spell Elantrovir taught him, knowing he needed to improve his control over it, but as his mood sank lower, he was more likely to find somewhere secluded, where he could simply sit and brood.

After three months, however, he experienced a moment of clarity while communing with the tanner's chickens: he must either leave and resume his search for a new master, or sink ever deeper into self-doubt and despondency. He had saved almost all of his wages, parting with little more than what was necessary to buy a suitable piece of leather from Voldin and pay a cobbler to make him a pair of shoes from it. Gorta had been good enough to outfit him with some of her sons' hand-me-downs (though they were still a bit big for him), and when he announced his intention to leave, Voldin made him a nice suede coin purse as a going-away present. He had a total of nine copper dragonets, one bronze falcon, four brass ferrets, and six tin starlings to put in it, as well as his five iron *nemtek*, but he exchanged five of the dragonets for a silver griffin, which he concealed in his belt along with his lock-picking tools. Being robbed had taught him not to take chances with his silver.

15

Piracy had become a serious menace to shipping by the late medieval period, as maritime trade picked up after centuries of stagnation. Pirate crews were notable for their ethnic diversity, as men of different races, eastern and western, were drawn together by their lust for treasure.

— Danger on the High Seas:
Piracy in the Medieval and Early Modern Eras

The night before his departure, Thonir washed all of his clothes with Gorta's strongest soap in the hope of purging them of tannery stink, and after breakfast the next morning, he said goodbye to the family. Gorta gave him a loaf of brown bread to keep his strength up, along with an old sack in which to carry it and his other few possessions. The three sons surprised him by actually speaking, while Voldin shook his hand, thanked him for his hard work, and advised him not to take any wooden falcons.

On his way to the docks, Thonir parted with a brass ferret and all of his tin starlings to purchase a bit of cheese and a few fresh vegetables to go along with the bread. He looked around him, pleased to be saying goodbye to Ksetilan and the Duchy of Hriss at last. The summer morning was already warm and the air humid. He hoped the Grand Duchy of Modir would have less oppressive weather. He was not sure how far up the coast it was, just that it lay some distance to the northwest.

The harbor was filled with ocean-going craft, but Thonir headed first for the largest and most impressive, an Esdiric carrack called the *Inskirekh-hasot,* or "Unicorn of the Sea" (a poetic Esdiric term for the narwhal). After one of the crewmen confirmed that the ship would be stopping at Modir on its way back to Esdiron, Thonir sought out the captain, a handsome if severe man of about forty, who expressed a willingness to take on a passenger for the right price, which he judged to be one silver griffin. Thonir offered three copper dragonets, and they compromised on four.

"We don't have much time before the tide turns against us," the captain told him in Esdiric, "so we're in a hurry. You just stay out of my men's way."

Thonir promised to cause no trouble, paid his four dragonets, and spent the time before the *Inskirekh-hasot* cast off exploring the magnificent three-masted vessel from stem to stern. Though smaller than the other two carracks he had seen recently, it was well constructed with a hull of Esdiric oak, coated with pitch. When Thonir descended to the lower deck, he encountered six marines, sharpening their swords, and a young man, reading a book by the light of his wand.

"Kholenakht!" said Thonir, once he had overcome his surprise.

The young man looked up and grinned. *"Dholenakht!"* he replied. Tall and thin, he had typical southern facial features, attractively arranged. His long dark hair was pulled into a ponytail, something Thonir would later learn was the current fashion among young unmarried Esdiric men. He was wearing an inexpensive brown cloak over similarly inexpensive brown clothes and shoes, suggesting somewhat straitened but still respectable circumstances.

"I did not expect to find a fellow wizard here," Thonir said in his best Esdiric.

The young man laughed. "Ghenrish the Humble Journeyman, at your service," he replied with an ironic bow of his head, "hired to protect and defend this glorious vessel and her fearless crew—just like my fellow mercenaries here." With a flourish he indicated the six marines, who looked up from their weapons and gave bored grunts of acknowledgment. Ghenrish smiled. "They don't say much, but they're happy to poke their swords into anyone who looks at them sideways, so I personally would advise against doing that."

Thonir did not understand everything Ghenrish had said, but he got most of it. "It is a pleasure to meet you," he said with the stilted formality of someone ill at ease with a foreign tongue. "I am Thonir, an even humbler apprentice— or at least I was until my master died." He had decided at the tannery to stop hiding behind a false name, and he saw no reason to resume doing so now. "I am going to Modir, where perhaps I find a new one. I hear a wizard named Khish lives there. Do you know him?"

Ghenrish made a face. "Only by reputation. A strange man, by all accounts. Paranoid. Volatile. I wouldn't want to study under him."

Thonir didn't know what the Esdiric words for "paranoid" and "volatile" meant, but he could tell from context that they could hardly be desirable qualities in a mentor. He felt his hopes deflate. "Is there someone else, some better wizard there in Modir?"

Ghenrish shook his head. "Haven't heard of anyone. You should go to Esdiron instead. I'm sure you could find a new master in Feldross. As the royal capital, it attracts wizards like rich heiresses attract suitors. I'd recommend the man who trained me, but he's very old. Old and tired. When I left, he said I was definitely the last apprentice he wanted to have anything to do with—ever." He laughed nostalgically. "Dear old Norshach! I'm afraid I gave the old geezer a lot of grief."

Hearing all of this left Thonir feeling discouraged again, but he asked Ghenrish the best way to get to Feldross regardless. The journeyman wizard explained that he should continue on from Modir to the Esdiric port of Shindesh and then proceed upriver. "Cheer up!" he added, encouragingly. "Feldross is a wonderful place."

The marines expressed agreement via a remarkable outpouring of profanity, only some of which Thonir understood from his exposure to Chodros. He nevertheless got the gist of their remarks, which was that the brothels in Feldross met with their wholehearted approval, although some thought the brothels in Shindesh were even better.

Ghenrish laughed again. "That wasn't exactly what I had in mind," he said, adding with a grin to Thonir, "which is not to say they're wrong!"

Thonir blushed. As in Karandoz, he found the idea of brothels simultaneously arousing and distasteful, for they brought his Asardian upbringing and his adolescent hormones into conflict. Asardianism, though by no means one of the more prudish sects in Ondiran, nevertheless frowned on reducing sexual intimacy to the status of a sordid commercial transaction. Thonir's sixteen-year-old body, however, had its own views on the subject, strong views. It was confusing.

Once the ship had left the harbor, the crew attended to some unpleasant business. Two sailors, both Inirochians, had failed to return to the ship that morning, forcing the captain to send out a search party, consisting of the six marines, who then found them—passed out drunk—in the alley behind one of the dockside taverns. The marines had roused the miscreants by shouts and some quick kicks to the ribs, and half-marched, half-carried them back to the ship, where the captain ordered them thrown into the hold to sober up prior to the infliction of exemplary punishment, which was now at hand.

Thonir watched as the two unfortunates were dragged on deck and strapped to the mainmast. Each of them received ten lashes, delivered by a particularly muscular sailor, who enjoyed his work and put his back into it. Hearing the crack of the whip and the screams of the victims was more than enough for Thonir, who turned away as the flogging began.

"You don't care for these maritime methods of castigation?" asked Ghenrish. "Nor do I, but the captain has to maintain discipline."

"Damn Rokies had it comin'," interjected one of the marines, using an Esdiric ethnic slur for Inirochians, "after makin' us waste our time goin' out lookin' for 'em."

"More to the point," Ghenrish noted, "they weren't here to help their shipmates this morning, when the schedule was already tight, forcing everybody else to work even harder."

Thonir shook his head. It was right to punish them, he thought, but not like this.

After the flogging, cheap wine was poured on the men's wounds, both to increase the pain and to prevent infection. Thonir wandered into the vicinity and covertly threw his anesthetizing spell on the two men. Concerned about depleting his *silendras,* he expended less upon them than he might have, but the magic still lessened their suffering.

Around noon, as the *Inskirekh-hasot* rounded the modest peninsula to the southwest of Ksetilan and turned northwest, word came down from the crow's nest that two caravels were approaching from further out to sea. Ghenrish swore—something about the horse-headed demons of Drindakh, if Thonir heard it right—and went over to the gunwale to look. "If those are pirates," he said with a sigh, "it will be time for me to earn my pay."

The marines retrieved crossbows from a storage locker, loaded them, and climbed onto the forecastle. Most of the sailors wore knives on their belts, but some now also grabbed boat hooks, with which they could fend off anyone attempting to board. The captain barked commands to the helmsman and the first mate from the poop deck.

The carrack was not a fast ship, and the two caravels rapidly closed the distance between them. They were flying black flags, in the approved piratical manner, and Thonir could see a team of archers readying their bows on the nearer vessel. He felt fear rising within him, bringing a hot flush to his face. He hastened to protect himself by erecting the invisible shield Elantrovir had taught him. The archers released their arrows in a volley, and one of these slammed harmlessly into Thonir's barrier. He was not sure it would have hit him in any case, but he was relieved that the spell had worked. Although most of the other arrows missed their targets, one sailor fell, mortally wounded, from a hit to the neck, while a second took one to the shoulder. The marines held their fire. Unlikely to have time to reload their cumbersome crossbows, they crouched low and waited until the pirates were closer. Ghenrish, on the other hand, did not hesitate. Having spotted the captain of the nearer ship, he dropped the man with a well-placed magical bolt to the chest.

A second volley of arrows arrived, felling another sailor.

Ghenrish swore again, but this time there was a palpable edge of fear to his voice. "May the gods save us," he told Thonir. "They've got a magician of their own, a thaumaturge by the look of him."

Now close to panic, Thonir saw him, too, on the further ship—a tall, bearded man, in black western dress, carrying a staff. Thaumaturgy, Thonir knew, was the magic system favored in the western lands. So far as he was aware, it was similar to wizardry and sorcery in scope and power but had its own mystical language and approach.

The thaumaturge had seen Ghenrish, too. He shook his staff at the wizard, who planted his feet and raised his wand in turn. A split-second later, amidst flying sparks and a tremendous crackle of electricity, the two men launched themselves into a long-range magical duel. Thonir stared open-mouthed, as the two mages sought to destroy each other with a brute-force application of naked magical power that was dazzling and terrifying both at once.

The first ship had now pulled alongside the carrack, however, prompting the marines to fire into the ranks of the archers, killing three just before they could release their third volley. The marines then dropped their crossbows and jumped down to the main deck, where pirates with grappling hooks were already trying to board and the carrack's sailors were using their boat hooks to dissuade them.

The magical duel did not last long. Older and more experienced than Ghenrish, the thaumaturge had learned to channel his *silendras* (or *sog-tir* in the mystical language of thaumaturgy) more efficiently, and he possessed slightly more innate ability to begin with. Had Thonir not been too frightened to think clearly, however, he would have realized that a dueling magician was uniquely vulnerable to attack by a third party. The boy thus missed his chance to break the thaumaturge's concentration and throw the match to his opponent. Instead, the duel grew ever more intense and the strain upon Ghenrish more visible, as his *silendras* waned, until finally an aneurysm burst in his brain. He gave a great cry, dropped his wand, and collapsed onto the deck.

For a brief moment, horror-fueled rage overcame Thonir's fear. Snatching up Ghenrish's wand, he hurled a fireball at the thaumaturge, who dispelled it with a disdainful flick of the wrist long before it could reach his ship and explode. The thaumaturge then lowered his staff at Thonir, who fell, unconscious, beside Ghenrish a moment later.

16

Slavery already had a distinct racial component by the late medieval period, with slavers providing mostly western captives to the east and mostly eastern ones to the west.

— *Everyday Life in the Middle Ages*

Thonir opened his eyes to total darkness, causing him to wonder briefly if he might be dead. On reflection, however, he concluded that an urgent need to urinate was unlikely to be a prominent feature of the afterlife, unless he had landed on a particularly low-rent plane of hell. Further, the soft moans of wounded men and muted conversations in Esdiric around him seemed unlikely to be the emanations of damned souls in torment, and while he found the atmosphere unpleasantly close, hot, and humid, the familiar rolling sensation he was experiencing convinced him he remained shipboard. He was also lying in perhaps half an inch of foul-smelling water. "Where are we?" he asked. "What's happening?"

"We're in the hold," replied a voice to his right.

"The pirates've taken the ship," explained another, to his left, "and locked us up down here."

"Those of us as survived the attack," clarified the first voice gloomily.

"How long ago?" asked Thonir. "How long have I been out?"

"Hard to tell time down here in the dark," pointed out the second voice, "but at least the better part o' the day."

Thonir's bladder reminded him of its needs. He groaned. "I have to pee."

"Well, for the gods' own sake, don't do it here," said the first voice. "Go aft. There's an old half-barrel we bin usin' there."

After a brief consultation with his neighbors to distinguish fore from aft in the dark, Thonir set out on his hands and knees, feeling his way past his fellow prisoners as best he could until he found the malodorous half-barrel in question. He had woken with a wide metal band around his neck, and once he had relieved himself, he investigated it. He was aware of an extraordinary sense of magical powerlessness—an utter absence of *silendras* he had never felt before, no matter how many spells he had cast or how exhausted he had been. With alarm, he realized that the metal band must be a "magician's collar" like the one the authorities had put on Chodros after his arrest to drain away his magical power. Feeling the band more carefully, he established that it was hinged at the back and fastened with some sort of locking mechanism at the front. He breathed a sigh of provisional relief. A lock was something he had a chance of picking.

Having crawled back to his starting point amidships, Thonir pumped the others for information, as he retrieved his tools from their hiding place in his belt and set to work. What he heard was not encouraging. The captain had gone down fighting, while the first mate had been brutally murdered shortly after he surrendered, leaving the second mate now in theoretical command of his fellow captives in the hold. Overall, the number of dead and wounded from the attack was considerable. As Thonir feared, Ghenrish had not survived.

"So, where do you think we're headed?" he asked. The intricate mechanism of the lock was proving troublesome.

"The Piratical Isles, for sure," said his first neighbor, a sailor named Khimor.

"Yup," said the second, the ship's carpenter, a man named Shomat. "Anybody worth ransoming, they'll hold onto. The rest of us'll end up in a stinkin' slave market somewhere west o' the sunset, as they say."

"Yeah, there's big demand for eastern slaves in the western lands," agreed Khimor. "Cruel people, them westerners, some of 'em."

"'Tain't like *we* treat slaves so good in Esdiron," objected a third man, whose name Thonir had yet to establish. "I'd rather be dead than a slave drainin' the marshes south of Feldross."

"Aw right, aw right," conceded Khimor irritably. "There's cruel people, some of 'em, both east *and* west. Happy now?"

Thonir made some adjustments to one of his picklocks and kept working. "How far is it to the Isles? How long have we got?"

"With the right winds, three, four days maybe," suggested Shomat. "More likely five or six. Either way, we're in this shithole of a hold for a good while yet."

Thonir felt the mechanism click. He gently pried the collar open and took it off. "Maybe," he said quietly, "maybe not."

The prospect of being sold into slavery, whether eastern or western, held no appeal for Thonir. Doing something to prevent it, therefore, was a prominent item on his personal agenda, though admittedly one in potential conflict with the first item, which was staying alive. Another important item, however, was letting his *silendras* replenish. Therefore, he tried to sleep, though it took some time for him to succeed. Being trapped in a hot, stuffy hold with a crowd of other people, while worrying about how to get out, overpower one's captors, and avoid being enslaved or killed, is not generally a situation conducive to nodding off. Ghenrish's death, too, weighed on the boy. He had liked the brash young Esdir, and watching the thaumaturge kill him had been traumatic. Nevertheless, Thonir *was* tired. Being rendered unconscious by magic had been no substitute for sleep, and eventually his thoughts dimmed, his body relaxed, and he began to doze.

When Thonir woke, several hours later, he felt somewhat restored. His *silendras* was not up to full strength after its complete draining by the magician's collar, but it had recovered sufficiently to give him some renewed confidence in his abilities, even if he still feared the dangerous task ahead. He began by casting a dim light spell on the deckhead (though it seemed quite bright at first to eyes grown accustomed to total darkness). Being able to see again provided a great boost to morale—not only his own, but also that of his fellow prisoners, who had mostly sunk into a state of despondent hopelessness. Discovering that they had someone among them who knew at least a little magic helped expand their sense of what might be possible.

Just as important, the light facilitated dispensing water from the two casks the pirates had allowed the prisoners to bring with them into the hold. In the dark, fair and adequate distribution had been all but impossible, and given the summer heat some of the crew were already suffering from dehydration.

Thonir sought out the second mate, an intelligent-looking man of about thirty, named Rishchik, who had sustained a knife wound to his left arm, now bandaged with a strip torn off his shirt. From their conversation, Thonir gathered that the pirates had transferred a skeleton crew to sail the *Inskirekh-hasot* to the Piratical Isles, while the two caravels resumed prowling the Hrissic coast. How large that skeleton crew might be, Rishchik could not say for certain.

"Must be at least ten," he hazarded, "but I'd hate to sail her with fewer than twenty." The *Inskirekh-hasot* had been carrying a crew of thirty-eight, not counting the marines.

"What if that thauma-what's-it of theirs is up there with 'em?" one of Rishchik's neighbors wanted to know.

"Then we're screwed," said Thonir bluntly. "If Ghenrish was no match for him, I certainly won't be."

"It wouldn't make much sense for him to stay aboard," Rishchik pointed out. "They won't be expecting any trouble from us, locked safely away down here, and they'll want his help if they find another ship to attack."

The discussion turned to the practicalities of getting out of the hold. The only means of egress was the large hatch in the low deckhead above. Its wooden cover was neither hinged nor locked, but the pirates had placed something heavy on it, making it impossible to lift from below.

"I should be able to shift it using magic," Thonir said, but I'll need more rest first."

Rishchik noted that the deck above, the orlop, was devoted solely to cargo. "There's no reason for the pirates to spend time on it, especially if they're stretched tight just sailing the ship. At any rate, I haven't heard anybody moving around up there." He considered the matter for a moment. "If we can get onto the orlop unnoticed, the captain stashed a few knives on it for times like this. From there, we'll have to climb through the main cargo hatch to get to the lower deck. It's a lot more likely we'll find pirates there, even if most of them'll be up on the weather decks."

Thonir nodded, trying to absorb all of this information in a foreign language. "How many men do you have—men who can fight?"

Rishchik sighed. "Well, four of the six marines bought it—most of them thanks to your friend the thaumaturge— but I think the other two would be up for any plan that'd let them kill pirates." He scratched his head. "By my count, we lost twelve out of our crew of thirty-eight. Another ten were wounded too badly to help us now—if they haven't pegged out in the meantime. So, that leaves sixteen, though some of us" (he held up his bandaged arm) "aren't in great shape, either. Not to mention that we won't have anything like enough weapons to go around."

Thonir frowned. "I'll try to—how do you say in Esdiric—odd the evens? No, even the odds, but I . . ." His voice trailed off. Remembering how frightened and useless he had been when the pirates attacked, he was afraid he would let everyone down when faced with them again. He clenched his jaw. "Well, I'll do what I can."

As they continued to elaborate their plan, Rishchik brought the boatswain and the two surviving marines into the discussion. There was only so much they could decide, however, given the many unknowns they faced. One indisputable fact was that they needed to wait for Thonir to regain more of his spell power. Balanced against this consideration, however, was the fact that the pirates had not provided the prisoners with any food, and there was no reason to think they would do so going forward. As a result, everyone was hungry, which made for impatience and short tempers. Rishchik was also concerned that their supply of water would not last many more days.

After several hours, Thonir felt as though he might be able to take a nap. He dispelled the light on the deckhead, so that if the pirates did open the hatch for some reason while he slept, they would not realize he had escaped his collar. When he woke up again, feeling much stronger, he relit the deckhead and told Rishchik he thought the time had come for them to make their final preparations.

Rishchik quickly organized their forces, gathering near the hatch all the men who would be conducting the assault. He briefly went over the plan, emphasizing the importance of carrying out its early phases in silence. Since only one man could climb through the hatch at a time, he lined them up in order, with the two marines at the front, followed by the boatswain, who was a tough, burly fellow, then the muscular sailor who had whipped the two Inirochians, and Shomat the carpenter. Thonir was to go sixth, although for the time being he was positioned out of line, directly beneath the hatch, where he could see what he was doing.

The representative of the merchant house that owned the ship, a well-fed, well-upholstered young man named Flochwik, declined to participate. "You're just going to get yourselves killed," he argued.

The carpenter had broken apart some heavy crates, so that each man had a piece of wood to use as an improvised weapon, and Thonir cast a light spell on six of these pieces, one for every third man, so they could see where they were going. Then he cast his levitation spell on the hatch cover, slowly lifting it—along with whatever was weighing it down—a few inches into the air. It was much heavier than an ingot of tin or pig iron, and he had to expend more *silendras* on the task than he would have liked. No light was visible through the cracks around it, suggesting that the orlop was in fact deserted. Thonir inched the cover to the side, just far enough for a man to climb through the hatch, and before he had even set it down again, the first marine had scrambled onto the orlop. The second quickly followed, and the line of men began to move. His legs quaking,

Thonir took his place behind Shomat, stepped onto the crate they had positioned below the hatch, and pulled himself through.

17

Long the subject of competing claims by the rulers of Tserenets, Ondiran, and Esdiron, the Fortunate Isles nevertheless maintained their independence for centuries under the control of pirate chieftains. The islanders are justly proud of this romantic heritage, and a pirate-themed festival is held each summer, attracting tourists from all over the world.

— A Visitor's Guide to the Fortunate Isles

Thonir got to his feet on the orlop and looked nervously up to the open cargo hatch in the deckhead. If anyone was amidships on the deck above, they could hardly fail to notice the magical light now emanating from below. Fortunately, the boatswain had already found and distributed the stash of four knives, and the two marines were racing up the ladders at either end of the long, rectangular hatch, blades clenched between their teeth, as though they were pirates themselves. The others followed, as the men behind them climbed up out of the hold.

The lower deck held no pirates amidships, but there were bulkheads fore and aft, and the two marines, once up their ladders, charged through the doors at either end. Unpleasant sounds issued from the galley, aft, as the second marine gutted a pirate he surprised there. The first marine found no one in the forward compartment, and both men waited for reinforcements before climbing the ladders to the fore and aft hatches, which led to fore and aft compartments on the main deck. The cargo hatch above was covered, with no ladders to reach it, so it would play no role in the assault.

Thonir, along with the boatswain, Shomat, Rishchik, and two other men, crowded into the galley, where the second marine was dragging the body of the pirate he had killed through the door leading to the tiny cabin normally shared by the ship's cook and his helper, where it would be out of the way. Once that task was accomplished, and Shomat had taken the dead man's knife, the second marine scaled the ladder and threw open the hatch leading to the cabin that Rishchik had shared with the first mate. This action woke a pirate napping in Rishchik's bunk, but the man scarcely had time to reach for his knife before the marine had slit his throat.

Once again, there was a pause, as the men behind caught up. After all, the door of the cabin would lead out into the open, where they could expect to find most of the remaining pirates. Rishchik, who had carefully thought through each stage of the assault, took the latest captured knife and gave the men their orders. Outside, on either side of the door, were steep steps up to the quarterdeck. The marine was to take the steps on the port side, the boatswain those on the starboard side, each of them followed by one of the two men Thonir did not know. Rishchik and Shomat would move out amidships, where they should meet up with their fellow crewmen emerging from the compartment beneath the forecastle. "Thonir," he said, "you stick with us. If you can, take up a central position, where you can hit them with spells from a safe distance. Stand with your back to the mainmast and don't forget to look for pirates in the rigging. Got it?"

Thonir nodded. He was not looking forward to this.

Thonir was the seventh person through the door, but by then Rishchik's plan had already gone awry. A pirate on the poop deck had picked up a cask and hurled it at the aft marine, as the latter tried to climb to the quarterdeck, knocking him off the portside steps and onto the man behind him. While the boatswain had succeeded in mounting the steps on the starboard side, two pirates on the quarterdeck were pressing him hard, preventing the man on the steps behind from joining him. Rishchik and Shomat were darting around either side of the mainmast to engage four more pirates amidships, on and around the cover of the cargo hatch. At the same time, the other marine and several crewmen—hearing battle joined—burst forth from the forward compartment, but in their eagerness to engage the four pirates on the deck in front of them, they overlooked the danger posed by two on the forecastle behind them. One of those pirates leaped off the forecastle, tackling a crewman, whom he grabbed by the hair and nearly decapitated with his knife as they went down. Meanwhile, two pirates were sliding down ropes in the rigging, one of them right on top of Thonir, who barely had time to conjure Elantrovir's invisible shield with a wild gesture of his hand. Thonir was thinking only to protect himself from the pirate's knife, but in his haste he cast the shield at a bit of an angle, which had the lucky consequence of deflecting the pirate himself into the sea, when the unsuspecting man crashed into the invisible barrier and lost his grip on the rope.

The fighting grew even more confused after that. Backing up against the ship's bulwarks, so that no one could get behind him, Thonir did succeed in putting two pirates to sleep and setting their leader's beard on fire, but afterward he would retain only scattered impressions of the desperate melee: the sailor Khimor hitting a pirate in the face with a piece of crate with nails sticking out of it; Rishchik sustaining another hit to his bandaged left arm; one of the marines breaking a pirate's neck after losing his knife. When it was all over, eight pirates were dead, three more were too badly wounded to continue fighting, two surrendered uninjured (including the pirate Thonir had knocked overboard), and two were captured magically asleep. Things were not much better on the winning side, however, for the pirates had succeeded in killing six more members of the crew, including the boatswain, and wounding five, including Rishchik and Shomat. Both marines were also badly hurt, which did not prevent them from killing the wounded pirates after they surrendered and abusing the others until Rishchik ordered them to stop.

Thonir was glad Rishchik did so, because he could not find the courage to intervene himself.

18

The collector should not be put off by the seeming complexity of medieval coinage. As almost every petty sovereignty in Ondiran issued its own coins, a certain amount of study is required for the novice to distinguish, say, a Sildooric silver shilling from a Hrissic silver griffin or a Rohliric silver decima—but the rewards of this engaging hobby are definitely worth it!

— Medieval Coins: How to Collect Them for Fun and Profit

Once the crew regained control of the ship, Rishchik ordered that the badly wounded crewmen who had remained in the hold during the assault be brought up to the lower deck, where their fellows could care for them—although three, as it turned out, had already died. He further ordered that the four surviving pirates—an Ondir, an Inirochian, and two westerners of some kind—be confined to the hold in their stead. The newly wounded, including Rishchik himself, also needed to be looked after, but the ship's surgeon had been killed in the pirates' initial attack, leaving the sailors to bind up each other's wounds as best they could. Thonir cast his anesthetizing spell on two men in particular pain.

While the ship's cook—one of the few crewmen who remained uninjured—hastily prepared food for his famished shipmates, Rishchik conferred with the navigator, a tall, swarthy man named Dhokh, on how to resume course to Modir. Judging from the position of the sun, it was late morning, so they had been sailing in the wrong direction for nearly a day, and the present unfavorable wind would slow their return. The crew trimmed the sails accordingly, but with so many men injured, the job took longer than it might have.

The next unhappy task was committing all the dead bodies to the deep. It made no sense to carry them back to the mainland in the summer heat, especially without any easy way to protect them from the ship's rats, which had already begun to sample the three in the hold. The burial prayers of various faiths were said, along with some heartfelt maledictions for the deceased pirates. Thonir said an Asardian prayer he remembered from childhood for Ghenrish, although the pirates had already dumped the wizard's body overboard the day before, along with the other dead from the initial attack.

The pirates had not touched the ship's cargo and left the crew's personal possessions largely undisturbed below decks, to be sorted and disposed of upon reaching the Piratical Isles. When they had thrown the survivors of their attack into the hold, however, the pirates stripped them of any belongings they might be carrying on their persons, especially coin purses, the contents of which were dumped into a strongbox for division later. Thonir therefore found the suede purse Voldin had given him in a pile of other empty purses on the orlop, near the hatch to the hold. After a little searching, he eventually found the sack he had brought aboard, as well, shoved into the forward compartment on the main deck, with Chodros's quill, Elantrovir's parchment, Gorta's loaf of bread, and the cheese and vegetables he had bought the morning before all still inside. He looked in vain for Ghenrish's wand and the small book the wizard had been reading when they met, but he was excited to find a traveling spell book under one of the bunks on the lower deck, along with a well-used straight razor and shaving brush. Thonir was not shaving yet, but he knew he would be soon, so he took both.

He also found a handsome emerald-green parrot, some ten inches from tip to tail, in the captain's cabin. Thonir had never seen a parrot before, or even heard of such a bird, but he was struck by its beautiful plumage and inquisitive eyes. Though initially leery of its powerful beak, he did not think the creature looked particularly savage, and when he said a cautious "Hello, there," he was astonished that it cocked its head to one side and replied, "Hello, there," with precisely the same intonation. "You can talk!" he exclaimed wonderingly, but the bird just looked at him for a moment and then said something in Inirochian that he could not understand—which was just as well, since it was patently offensive. Living among pirates had equipped the bird with a lively multilingual vocabulary.

Thonir was fond of animals, but Chodros had taken a dim view of them and never allowed him to keep a pet. The boy slowly stretched out his right hand, and after an appraising look the bird hopped onto it. "Mizzenmast," it said irrelevantly in Esdiric and began to climb up his arm to perch on his shoulder. Thonir had not foreseen this move, but he quickly concluded that the bird had no hostile intent and held his arm out straight to facilitate its ascent. "Man the yard," the bird said, in Ondiric this time.

"You're quite a fine bird," Thonir remarked. "I wonder what I should call you." He stroked the feathers on the parrot's breast cautiously with one finger, and it swished its tail appreciatively.

"Salty dog," the bird declared. "No safe haven. Give no quarter."

Thonir laughed. "You're quite a chatterbox, aren't you. Yes, I think I'll call you Kwirimak—I'll have to make sure, but I believe that's the Esdiric word for *chatterbox*."

"Chatterbox," repeated the bird, bobbing its head up and down. "Pretty parrot demon-spawn."

Rishchik ordered that all the money the pirates had been carrying be added to the strongbox of stolen coins. Assisted by Dhokh, and watched by several other sharp-eyed members of the crew, he then counted all 492 coins in the box. Most were from Esdiron, but five of the Inirochian city states were also represented, as were six different Ondiric sovereignties, the Kingdom of Tserenets, three suzerainties of the great western Phomentic Empire, and even the remote western Satrapy of Vi'oor. With the exception of four gold coins, however, which indisputably belonged to Flochwik, the merchants' representative, there was no way to establish reliably who owned any of them. Rishchik therefore decreed that the rest would be divided evenly amongst the survivors and the families of the deceased, and—after much calculating of their value—determined that each share consisted of one Esdiric silver *poog*, six copper *tesh*, and five copper *sirk*. Flochwik protested that his purse—in addition to the four gold coins—

135

had contained six silver pieces and eight copper, but Rishchik retorted that since the man had taken no part in the fighting, he should be glad to receive anything at all. Rishchik pointed out that his own purse had contained four silver coins, but he claimed no more than his equal share. The two marines grumbled that they deserved a larger cut, but Rishchik promised to press the merchant house to bestow a separate bonus upon them for their good service. Given the complexity of working out an equitable division of the extraordinarily varied coinage in the strongbox, distribution would in any case have to await the ship's return to its home base of Shindesh, where the money could be paid wholly in Esdiric currency.

Thonir slept soundly that night, with Quirinak (as the name is correctly rendered) perched companionably on his bunk. In the morning, the boy let the bird climb onto his shoulder and together they went up to the main deck, where the sails were hanging limp.

"We've been becalmed since midnight," Rishchik told him. "Our progress yesterday was slow, but we did make it far enough that you can see the Hrissic coast off to starboard now. I'd say it's maybe another twenty miles to Ksetilan—but until the wind picks up, we're adrift."

"We're adrift," repeated Quririnak, mimicking Rishchik precisely.

The air remained still for the better part of two days. Fortunately, the ship was well stocked with food and water, and there were of course fewer mouths to feed now, but the lack of adequate medical care continued to be a serious problem. Several men's wounds became infected, and one man died during the second night after developing a terrible fever.

Under the circumstances Thonir felt obliged to do a little amateur nursing, but he spent most of his time studying Ghenrish's spell book. As a work designed to be carried on the wizard's travels, it held a carefully curated selection of spells Ghenrish had not felt a need to memorize but still deemed potentially useful. Several were specific to seafaring, such as magicks to plug leaks, alleviate seasickness, or render saltwater potable. Only a handful were spells Chodros had taught Thonir, and none were spells the boy knew by heart, so all of them added to his magical arsenal.

Of course, Thonir also spent time getting to know his parrot—familiarizing himself with its psittacine habits, teaching it new words, and feeding it nuts and seeds from a stash he had found in the captain's cabin. He was pleased to find that Quirinak was affectionate, playful, and remarkably intelligent, with strong opinions on certain subjects. Unsure whether it was male or female, he ultimately decided that—not being a parrot himself—its sex did not matter very much to him. He was, in any case, inclined to think the bird might resent a close inspection of its genitalia.

The wind picked up in mid-afternoon on the second day, enabling them to reach Ksetilan by early evening. As the crew docked the ship, Rishchik asked Thonir if he knew how to open locks by magic. "I need to get into the box the captain used for payroll," he explained, "and the pirates must have dumped the key along with his body."

Thonir accompanied Rishchik and Dhokh to the captain's cabin, where Rishchik dragged an iron box out from under the captain's bunk. Just to be on the safe side, Thonir cast a spell to detect any enchantment on it, but there was none, so he went ahead and magicked open the lock. Rishchik thanked him, removed a quantity of silver, and carried the box out onto the quarterdeck.

"I'm going ashore to secure the services of a healer," he announced to the crew. "While I'm gone, I am charging Dhokh here with distributing your pay. You are free to go ashore yourselves, but anyone too drunk or hung-over to work in the morning will receive five lashes. We're far too shorthanded for anyone to shirk his duties. That said, we'll take on more hands here, if we can—so if you do leave the ship, spread the word that we're hiring." He turned to Thonir. "You come with me. I don't speak Ondiric very well, and it's vital we convince a healer to come and tend our wounded." He paused. "Oh, and leave that damned parrot behind!"

Consultation in a dockside tavern yielded directions to the home of a healer named Nomintar, a short distance away. A western girl of about seventeen answered their knock. "Yes?" she asked. Though not pretty, she had a gentle voice and kind eyes.

Thonir felt suddenly self-conscious. "Um, yes, uh, hello, er, miss," he stammered. He took a deep breath and tried again. "We seek the healer Nomintar. Our ship was attacked by pirates, and there are many wounded. Please, we need help!"

The girl nodded. "I see, yes, of course." Despite her western features, her dress was cut in the Ondiric style, and she spoke with no trace of a western accent. "One moment." As she turned, a long-limbed man with ashen hair and gray-blue eyes came up behind her in the traditional green robes of a healer.

"How many people are hurt?" he demanded. Notwithstanding his Ondiric name, he spoke with a slight foreign accent Thonir did not recognize.

"Fourteen," replied Thonir, "some very badly. Several have fevers."

"Bandages, Irinitsi," the healer said crisply. He looked critically at the bloody rags wrapped around Rishchik's arm. "Lots of bandages, all the catgut we have, and a bottle of my fever draft."

"Yes, Eminence," the girl replied dutifully and went to fetch these items.

The healer gestured for Thonir and Rishchik to wait on the doorstep, as he retrieved a bag from another room. Irinitsi rejoined them shortly, bearing a bundle, which Thonir volunteered to carry for her.

Fortunately, Nomintar spoke some Esdiric, so he did not need an interpreter to communicate with Rishchik on the way back to the ship. Both men were tall, and they took long strides, while Thonir and Irinitsi, who were shorter, struggled to keep up.

Thonir was glad that the bundle, while cumbersome, was not heavy. "You are Nomintar's apprentice then?" he asked shyly.

Irinitsi nodded. "One more year and I hope to have earned my healer's robes."

Squelching an impulse to tell her about the woeful truncation of his own apprenticeship, Thonir asked instead for more information about healing, and in the short time it took to reach the docks, he relaxed considerably, finding Irinitsi an interesting and pleasant companion.

⚜

On the lower deck, the light of a few tallow candles flickered over the wounded men in their bunks.

"Light up the deckhead, will you, Thonir?" requested Rishchik. "The healers need decent illumination." He turned to an unwounded sailor. "Fetch some water. They'll need that, too."

Thonir cast his light spell. Irinitsi looked surprised but said nothing. Instead, she and Nomintar set efficiently to work, cleaning, debriding, and suturing the men's wounds. Nomintar packed infected cuts with an herb from his bag, and gave febrile patients a dose of his fever draft. Thonir did what he could to assist Irinitsi, who gave him a medicinal salve she had brought along to apply to abrasions. When men were in serious pain, he cast his anesthetizing spell.

After the healers had attended to the most badly wounded men—by which time it was quite late—the walking wounded were brought down from the weather decks, where most of them were sleeping. Rishchik refused

140

treatment for his own wounded arm until the healers had finished tending to his men. He then paid Nomintar with the silver he had taken from the payroll box and—together with Thonir and the two marines—escorted the healers safely home through the darkness of night. Thonir was sorry to say goodbye to Irinitsi, who had impressed him with her combined gentleness and skill. The girl might not be pretty, he told himself, but she did have a pleasing smile.

The *Inskirekh-hasot* spent the next two days in Ksetilan, for Rishchik was unwilling to leave before he had taken on at least five new deckhands. He also turned the captured pirates over to the Hrissic authorities during this time and gave a witness statement—as did Dhokh and Flochwik—to be used at their trial. Thonir continued to study Ghenrish's spell book, devoting particular attention to the idiosyncrasies of the wizard's handwriting. Though Ghenrish had written legibly enough for the most part, he formed certain letters in odd ways, and Thonir knew that misreading an incantation could have alarming consequences.

On the second day, Nomintar sent Irinitsi to check on the wounded. The girl changed a few dressings and administered some fever drafts but declared herself largely satisfied with the men's progress. Glad to see her again, Thonir hung around and asked what he hoped were intelligent questions about wound care. She in turn admired his parrot and had a few questions for him about wizardry. In the end he walked her home. He learned that she was an ethnic Djaswir, one of the many peoples of the Phomentic

Empire, though she herself had been born and raised in Ksetilan. "My parents returned home last year," she said sadly, as they neared her master's abode. "They want me to join them once I've finished my apprenticeship, but I'm not sure I want to go."

Thonir made sympathetic noises. He was just working his way up to proposing that they have lunch together, when Irinitsi said goodbye and vanished into the house.

19

Import and export duties reached preposterous heights under Choofren III and Nishgok IX, hampering trade and causing smuggling to flourish across every land and sea border.

— An Economic History of Esdiron, vol. 1

The journey to Modir was mercifully uneventful, and the *Inskirekh-hasot* docked in the grand duchy's busy harbor after only a day and a half at sea. Having abandoned his plan to contact the "paranoid" and "volatile" wizard Khish, Thonir instead helped to unload the ship's partial cargo of flax (leaving several hundredweight of copper for delivery to Esdiron) and then to load a number of bolts of fine linen and slabs of beeswax in its place. The merchant house that owned the ship had a branch office in Modir with which Flochwik coordinated to take care of all the arrangements and pay the customs duty, so the entire process was completed in time for the ship to cast off again shortly before dark. The merchant house also provided another eight marines in case of further pirate trouble.

The next leg of the voyage, however, brought home to Thonir that sea serpents and pirates were not the only dangers facing seafarers. Though the winds were favorable the first night, the sky grew threatening by morning, and a fierce storm broke out in early afternoon. As a carrack, the *Inskirekh-hasot* was a broad-beamed vessel, with greater stability in heavy seas than narrower craft, but Thonir could be forgiven for failing to appreciate this relative advantage, once the storm began to show what it could do, pitching and rolling the ship with extraordinary force, heaving it to the crest of each new wave, and then crashing it to the depth of the trough. The boy did his best to wedge himself and his belongings into his bunk, while he listened to the shriek of the gale, the crack of the thunder, and the shiver of the ship's timbers, fully expecting the vessel to come to pieces at any moment. Less able to hold on, some of the wounded crewmen around him were thrown repeatedly from their own bunks, smashing into the decking, bulkheads, or whatever else hard and painful might be nearby. To make matters worse, anything that had not been battened down took flight and became a menace. A chair thus smashed into the framework of Thonir's bunk at one point, and a loose bottle struck him painfully on the knee a bit later. Quirinak, who had lived through worse storms, made a great deal of noise but managed to avoid injury.

Thonir was not expecting to suffer from seasickness. After his initial light nausea aboard the *Porpoise,* he had enjoyed good fortune in this regard, but now he spewed more vomit than he had ever realized any one person could have at their disposal. Once the worst of it was out of him, he struggled to open Ghenrish's book and find its spell to counter the affliction, for the dry heaves, he knew, were the worst.

By the time the storm abated, several hours later, Thonir was exhausted. He had acquired any number of bruises. His clothes were soiled with vomit. He wanted to stay in his bunk and nap, but the ship had taken on water during the storm. While the others manned the bilge pumps, he expended the last of his flagging *silendras* to plug the leaks, using the spell for that purpose from Ghenrish's book. As a result, he was unable to anesthetize a sailor's broken arm, or even to cleanse his own clothes and bunk, and of course there was nothing anyone could do about one of the new deckhands, who had been swept overboard and lost.

The *Inskirekh-hasot* reached Shindesh two days later. The first order of business was a visit by Rishchik and Flochwik to their employers at the Merchant House of Ghilgesh, accompanied by Dhokh and Thonir at Rishchik's request. The first three, who intended to return to the ship, knew better than to bring anything of value with them—apart from the strongbox of coins, which Dhokh was carrying— but Thonir, who expected to be on his way after receiving his share of the money, gathered his belongings and brought them along.

"Hold hard, you four!" barked a grim-faced Esdiric customs inspector, as they came down the gangplank. Some five yards behind him, two soldiers in leather armor planted their feet in a broad stance and crossed their glaives, blocking exit from the pier. "Strongbox, metal: one *tesh*," the inspector said, pointing, as he approached. "Open it!"

Dhokh put down the box and opened the lid. The customs inspector satisfied himself that it contained only coins. "Specie, various: no *import* duty," he said, stressing the word significantly (for Esdiron had a special ten-percent export duty on coins to discourage people from taking them out of the country). He removed one *tesh* from the box and placed it in a pouch bearing the royal seal of Esdiron. He pointed to Quirinak. "Plumage bird, exotic: one *poog*."

"Balderdash!" said the parrot.

"Plumage bird, exotic *talking*: one *poog*, three *tesh*," the customs inspector corrected himself.

"Aargh!" screamed the parrot.

The customs inspector pointed again. "What's in that sack?"

Thonir opened the sack containing most of his belongings, including the "magician's collar," which he had retrieved from the hold while he was plugging leaks. Fortunately, the customs inspector did not recognize it as magical.

"Collar, metal, non-precious—dutiable as costume jewelry: three *tesh*." The inspector gestured toward a knife Thonir had taken from one of the dead pirates. "Edged weapon with sheath: one *poog*. Razor, straight, with shaving brush: seven *tesh*. Quill pen: one *sirk*. What's that book under your arm?"

Growing more incredulous by the second, Thonir showed him. Elantrovir's parchment was tucked inside.

The customs inspector examined both. "Writings in magical script: two *poog*. Turn out your pockets."

Evidently there was no tariff on small pieces of string, bits of fluff, or half-eaten slices of brown bread.

"Total duty: five *poog*, one *tesh*, one *sirk*."

Thonir was flabbergasted. "I don't have that much money!" he objected. He held out his empty coin purse. "See? I don't have *any* money!"

"Fine for refusal to pay due to insufficiency of funds: one *sirk* per *tesh*," said the inspector in a bored tone, casting his eyes skyward, as he did some mental calculations. "That's another . . . ten *tesh*, one *sirk*, for a total due of five *poog*, eleven *tesh*, two *sirk*."

Thonir felt trapped. "This is madness!" he pleaded.

"Madness!" repeated the parrot.

Rishchik attempted to intervene. "There's no need for a fine, Inspector. The House of Ghilgesh will pay the boy's duty. Won't it, Flochwik." There was no hint of a question in his intonation.

When Flochwik hesitated, Dhokh cut in: "If it warn't for this boy's gettin' us outta that stinkin' hold, the House of freakin' Ghilgesh would be out a fully loaded carrack—and *you*, you'd be in a pirate cell by now, sittin' on yer sorry arse waitin' t'find out if yer fancy bosses think it's worth ransomin'."

Flochwik looked uncomfortable. "Perhaps we could *advance* him the money," he conceded.

This brief interlude gave Thonir a moment to calm down and consider his options. He had no wish to be indebted five or six silver pieces to the House of Ghilgesh. He preferred instead to cast a quiet charm spell on the customs inspector, pouring more *silendras* into it than he had ever put into such a spell before. "There is no need for the merchant house to be involved," he said. *There is no need for any of this at all!* "This good man, he made a small mistake in his cal-, calc-, er, his figures," he explained, stumbling over the Esdiric word. He turned to the customs inspector. *Everyone makes mistakes, Inspector. We don't want to get an honest man like you in trouble over it.* "One *tesh* is all we owe, and already we paid that. Is that not right, Inspector?"

The man looked flustered. "Yes, it appears so. A simple error. I do apologize."

Thonir breathed a sigh of relief. "Thank you, Inspector. Good day to you." *Now, signal those nice soldiers to let us pass!*

The soldiers uncrossed their glaives and stood at ease, allowing them off the pier. As they headed for the merchant house, Rishchik laughed and slapped Thonir on the back. "Nicely handled, kid. Good to see someone make a fool of one of our glorious customs men for once!"

The Merchant House of Ghilgesh was a family enterprise, now run by its second generation—though one first-generation founder remained above ground and sometimes still saw fit to interfere. The firm had established itself by trading in grain during a great famine but quickly branched out into other commodities, manufactures, or indeed almost anything that might turn a profit, sometimes including slaves, though fortunately not often. Its headquarters—rendered in a particularly overwrought variation on a recently expired architectural fashion—stood near the city's central market square, a monument to the social striving and questionable taste of the firm's founders and their wives.

Flochwik, as a mere nephew of the spouse of one of the less enterprising current partners, held a correspondingly subordinate position in the firm, but his return to base with the *Inskirekh-hasot* warranted a full report to persons of greater consequence, who forgathered upon news of his arrival to hear it. He spoke at length, somehow managing to paint a flattering portrait of his own negligible role in retaking the ship, while downplaying Rishchik's demonstrated leadership.

Thonir found this presentation infuriating but sensed it was not his place to protest. He could tell that Dhokh shared his feelings, but the navigator kept his mouth shut, limiting himself to a display of disapproving body language.

When Flochwik finished, Rishchik made no attempt to correct the record, focusing instead on the need to obtain further medical attention for the wounded, to arrange the equitable division of the cash in the strongbox, and to grant bonuses to the surviving marines. He concluded by praising Thonir's contribution, as well, suggesting that the boy also receive some reward for his part in saving the ship.

Dhokh maintained his silence but nodded vigorously.

Somewhat to Thonir's surprise, Flochwik did not demur. "The boy did well," he acknowledged. "He also showed quick thinking today, when he bamboozled a customs inspector. I submit that hiring him to use his magicks to thwart the absurd and punitive exactions of our customs and excise men would be both a suitable reward for his past actions and a profitable proposition for ourselves."

The most senior of the merchants, a rotund, richly attired man well into middle age, wanted more details. "What sort of magic did you employ upon this customs official?" he asked. "Could you use it more widely to our advantage?"

Thonir cleared his throat nervously. "It was a wizarding charm, Master Merchant. It bent him to my will, so he charged me no duty. The spell does not always work, though. Men can learn to resist it. But there is also another spell . . ." (he hesitated, not knowing the Esdiric word for *befuddle*), "a spell that confuses the mind, makes a man lose his thoughts for a time and become simple. Under the influence of one of these spells or the other, customs men should give you little trouble."

"Little trouble," affirmed Quirinak.

One of the younger merchants, a sharp-eyed man with his hair in a neat ponytail, shook his head. "I think we need proof of this."

Thonir shrugged. "As you like." He cast his befuddling spell on the fellow, whose jaw went slack and eyes grew vacant. He then walked over to him and took the man's purse from his belt, before taking several steps away and releasing him from the spell. "Catch!" he said, tossing him back the purse.

The other merchants laughed. "He got you there, cousin," one of them chortled.

"I think the boy's power is adequately demonstrated," said the senior merchant. "Are we agreed?" Hearing no dissents, he continued: "I propose we pay this boy six *poog* for each customs inspection he thwarts. Is that acceptable?" He turned to Thonir. "We own eight ships, which come and go regularly from the harbor here. That should give you quite a nice little income."

Placing his hand on Thonir's shoulder, Rishchik protested: "Inspections of the *Inskirekh-hasot* run anywhere from twelve to twenty gold *troog*, depending on the cargo. Six silver *poog* is but a small fraction of the money he'll save you."

The senior merchant frowned. "Most of our ships are smaller than the *Inskirekh,* but very well then, eight *poog* per inspection."

Thonir tried to take it in. Eight silver pieces. He was not sure precisely how much a *poog* was worth, but he was under the impression that it was roughly comparable to a silver griffin. Given the boy's impecunious frame of reference, eight *poog* was a vast sum—as much as he would have made working in the tannery had he remained there for over nine months. Admittedly, the work being proposed was illegal, but his encounter with the extortionate Esdiric customs regime that day had shocked him sufficiently to make him question whether it was actually *wrong.* He stepped forward and shook hands with the senior merchant. "I accept."

Before they could return to the ship, the matter of the strongbox and its contents required resolution. Although Flochwik grudgingly attested to the correctness of Rishchik's valuation of its contents, the merchants insisted that their treasurer confirm it. After sorting out and counting all the coins, this person valued a few of the foreign ones at a slightly lower rate than Rishchik had done, producing a slightly lower total (and of course the customs inspector had removed one *tesh),* but the result was not enough lower that she chose to contest the amount Rishchik had promised everyone. They went over the crew manifest, on which Rishchik had noted those crewmen who had been killed and which now would be used to record the distribution of the money. Flochwik's name and Thonir's were therefore added to the bottom. The treasurer counted out their shares, as well as Rishchik's and Dhokh's, and each one signed by his name to acknowledge receipt.

All of this took no small amount of time, but Thonir had no complaints, for the firm's treasurer was an attractive young woman with lustrous auburn hair, in whose proximity he was happy to remain indefinitely. Her name was Oshintil, and she addressed the senior merchant as "cousin" and one of the younger ones as "brother," leading Thonir to conclude that she must herself be a member of the merchant family. Like the others, she was expensively attired, and her dress was skillfully cut to accentuate her figure, making it all the more difficult for Thonir to take his eyes off her.

Once these important matters had been sorted out, Flochwik arranged for several of the firm's wagons to accompany them back to the ship. On the way he also stopped to engage a gang of dockworkers to help with the unloading, as the crewmen were in no condition to handle the job alone.

Using his befuddling spell to render the customs inspectors helpless to resist the charm that followed, Thonir successfully kept at zero the duty assessed on the carrack's load of copper, linen, and beeswax. Afterward he and Flochwik returned to the Merchant House, accompanied by almost all the crewmen who could walk, for they were eager to claim their share of the strongbox money. Rishchik came along, as well, intent on making arrangements on behalf of the families of those who had not survived.

Oshintil counted out Thonir's eight *poog* and recorded it in her ledger.

"Be sure she's given you coins minted before the current reign," warned Rishchik, "before the bastards in the royal treasury began to debase the currency."

Oshintil tossed her head. "Always so mistrustful! When have I ever cheated you, Rishchik?" She fished a coin out of her till and showed it to Thonir. "This is what you want to watch out for. HRH CH III. His Royal Highness Choofren III. Worth only eight to ten *tesh* instead of twelve, depending on how much base metal they've mixed in with the silver."

Thonir thanked her. "How will I know when you have another customs inspection?" He spoke slowly and carefully, anxious not to look foolish by making mistakes in grammar or usage.

She smiled. "Let us know where you're staying, and we'll send Glip."

He gave her a puzzled look. "Glip?" It did not sound like an Esdiric name.

"Glip?" repeated Quirinak with a tilt of the head.

Oshintil laughed. "Glip, our messenger boy."

Thonir thanked her again. Unable to think of an excuse for remaining while the crewmen claimed their money, he reluctantly took his leave. Besides, he needed to find some supper and a place to spend the night.

20

Located on the River Shin, Shindesh is Esdiron's second-largest city and her preeminent seaport. Despite the loss of most relics of the past in a disastrous fire some sixty years ago, there is much to see and do. Given its unsavory reputation, however, the Penshin District adjacent to the docks is best avoided by respectable visitors.

— *The Motor-Tourist's Guide to Esdiron* (1st ed.)

Thonir was glad he had memorized Trofim's spell to eradicate bloodsucking vermin, for the inn at which he stayed that night was badly infested. Having the money to afford a tiny room of his own was pleasant, however, and he took advantage of the privacy to stash most of the silver *poog* he had obtained that day in his belt, alongside the silver griffin he had secreted there back in Ksetilan.

He spent much of the next day exploring Shindesh, as he searched for longer-term accommodations. It was the biggest city he had seen to date, markedly Esdiric in its architecture, street life, and general ambiance. Being unimpressed by the seedy boarding houses near the docks, he decided to look for a nice room in a private home. Not everyone was willing to take a tenant with a parrot, but he eventually found a room he liked in a comfortable old house owned by a middle-aged widow named Madam Shabiril, who took to Quirinak at once. The bird reciprocated her interest, giving a raucous squawk that Thonir had already identified as signifying approval, and refraining from saying anything palpably obscene. Thonir was particularly pleased to have found someone who liked the parrot, for he had already concluded that he would need to leave Quirinak at home when out on business for the merchant house. He needed to remain inconspicuous, and having a talkative emerald-green parrot on his shoulder was the opposite of that.

❦

After paying in advance for a week's lodging plus two meals per day, Thonir returned to the merchant house to tell Oshintil where he was staying. The young woman was wearing an even more eye-catching dress than the day before, rendering the boy slightly giddy, but he managed to convey his news without making a complete fool of himself. After a moment's hesitation, he added: "What Flochwik said yesterday—about how he helped retake the ship—that wasn't right. He stayed in the hold until it was safe to come out."

"Oh, Flochwik," she snorted. "I know better than to believe half of what *he* says."

Encouraged, Thonir continued. "It was Rishchik who deserved the, um, the—" He gave up trying to remember the Esdiric word for *credit*. "Deserved the praise."

Oshintil smiled. "But *you* were the one who got everyone out of the hold, weren't you?"

Thonir blushed, pleased she had registered this important detail. "Well, yes," he admitted. "But Rishchik planned our attack. He led it. Even though he was already hurt. And afterward he got us back safe to port. I just thought someone

155

here should know. I mean, he told everyone that the marines should get something extra, that I should get something, but he is the one who really should. Talk to Dhokh, or any of the crewmen, really. They will speak for him."

Oshintil nodded. "Don't worry. I'll mention it to the others." She smiled again. "It's nice of you to stick up for your friend."

Thonir blushed anew. "Thank you, miss. He sticked, er, stuck up for me."

✦

Thonir had not given up on finding a wizard to continue his training. While waiting for word of a new customs inspection to thwart, he looked into his options in Shindesh. As it happened, there was a highly accomplished wizard on the municipal payroll, but the man already had an apprentice, who met Thonir's inquiries with undisguised hostility. There were also two freelance wizards in town, but one disclaimed having the experience to take on an apprentice, while the other disparaged Thonir's ethnic origin. "I ain't training no Ondir trash," he growled, as he turned the boy away.

✦

Four days after Thonir arrived in Shindesh, a western boy of about twelve came looking for him at Madam Shabiril's first thing in the morning.

"They got a job for you down at the docks," the boy said. He spoke Esdiric with no trace of a western accent. "Wow, nice parrot!"

156

"Thanks," said Thonir. "His name's Quirinak. So, you must be Glip."

The boy confirmed this. "Gli'ipiramavintsi'i, really," he said, "but everybody here just calls me Glip."

"Gli'ipiramavintsi'i," repeated Quirinak, who was always up to a challenge.

"Where are you from then?" asked Thonir.

"Ni'ontimoria," the boy replied. In response to a blank look from Thonir, he added, "That's in the Phomentic Empire." He reached out tentatively to pet Quirinak, who responded with enthusiasm. "But pirates got me when I was eight, an' sold me to the merchants."

"I'm sorry. Do they treat you all right, the merchants?"

"Mostly. Some of 'em are nicer than others."

"Yes, I can imagine." Thonir produced a copper *sirk* and laid it on the table. "Tell me about them. Just who am I working for?"

Glip slid the coin off the table and into his pocket. He was happy enough to gossip about his masters, telling Thonir which ones drank, who beat his wife, and who had a morbid fear of donkeys.

"Tell me about Oshintil," urged Thonir.

Glip smirked. He might be only twelve, but he readily grasped the nature of the older boy's interest. "A peach, ain't she," he replied. "Clever, too. A real head for figures, that one. And she treats me good. Never hits me, anyway."

Thonir made ready to leave. He placed another *sirk* on the table. "Tell me more as we go."

By the time they reached the merchant house, Thonir had learned that Oshintil was twenty-two, the youngest member of the family's second generation, and under pressure to marry the scion of an allied merchant house.

"She don't like him, though," said Glip, "and Mistress Oshi, she's used to doin' just as she likes."

From the merchant house, Thonir followed an Esdiric sea captain to the docks, where a cog named the *Fir-shiranto,* or "Spiny Dogfish," awaited. He had no difficulty frustrating the customs inspection, and the crew then unloaded a fortune in western spices, silks, and carpets, all duty-free. Afterward, back at the merchant house, the captain attested to Thonir's success, and Oshintil smilingly dispensed eight more silver *poog.* The young woman had braided her hair in an elegant updo Thonir thought very becoming, though he did not quite have the nerve to tell her so.

Over the following days, as he waited for his next assignment, Thonir spent much of his time with Rishchik and Dhokh, who were recruiting sailors to replenish the badly depleted crew of the *Inskirekh-hasot,* as well as waiting for the merchant house to find the ship a new captain. Thonir thought the job should go to Rishchik himself, but the young man just laughed and said he was content with having been promoted to first mate.

One advantage of hanging around with Rishchik, Thonir discovered, was that his friend's determination to see the families of the dead crewmen receive the money due to them meant he attended repeatedly upon Oshintil at the merchant house, and Thonir's crush on the lovely treasurer deepened with every visit. Soon he was thinking about her almost constantly, while closing his mind to any possible flaws in her personality or character. At the same time, he was perfectly well aware that she was six years older than he was, belonged to a wealthy merchant family, and must necessarily regard him as the callow youth he in fact knew himself to be. He therefore resigned himself to worshipping her from afar—or if not quite from afar, then at least from a safe middle-distance. He was particularly frustrated that he could not sing her praises to Quirinak, for he was certain the loquacious bird would choose the most embarrassing possible moment to repeat anything he might say.

A carrack was far too valuable a property to go to sea without magical protection, so the *Inskirekh-hasot* remained in port even after a captain was found, until a wizard could come downriver from the Esdiric capital to take up the post formerly held by Ghenrish. This happened a day after the autumnal equinox. He was a young man, no older than twenty-one, with a studious face, a slight squint, and a large black tomcat. Thonir was glad not to have brought Quirinak, who seemed unlikely to approve of cats.

In any event, Thonir felt he had to warn the ship's new wizard about the thaumaturge. "Be careful," he urged. "He's very strong, so don't let him draw you into a duel. If you do, he will kill you. So, if you meet pirates, wait until he shows himself. Then you can—what's your Esdiric phrase?—*get the jump* on him. Don't think you have to fight fair with this bastard. Stay out of sight until you can drop him with a spell he won't see coming."

Rishchik laughed. "Listen to the boy. He knows what he's talking about."

The young wizard nodded gravely. "Yes, it sounds like he does."

At this point two weasel-eyed fellows wearing the yellow jerkins of the Royal Esdiric Customs Inspectorate arrived, followed at a respectful distance by two soldiers. Rishchik welcomed the inspectors aboard and introduced them to the captain. Thonir then cast his befuddling spell on them, followed by a charm. Having given the matter some thought, he had come to the conclusion that simply sending inspectors away every time would become dangerous, so he had studied the detailed schedule of goods posted outside the customs house and come up with a few things that incurred little or no duty.

Accordingly, he praised the newly arrived inspectors for having conducted such a thorough and conscientious inspection, in which they had determined that the *Inskirekh-hasot* was carrying nothing but duty-free low-quality sand for export to Ondiran. The inspectors then duly recorded the purported cargo in their ledger, shook their heads, and marveled at those Ondiric fools, who were prepared to pay good money for something available for nothing on any beach. Doing his best to keep a straight face, Thonir agreed that the Ondir were a foolish people, with no proper conception of modern business methods.

Once the inspectors departed, Thonir went with Rishchik to collect his pay at the merchant house, where they found that Oshintil had changed her hairstyle again. Thonir thought she looked ravishing, but Rishchik saw fit to tease her about this propensity to alter her appearance. It might come in handy one day, he suggested, when the royal customs authorities cracked down on the House of Ghilgesh and she had to "go on the lam," as he put it, an expression that was new to Thonir. Although Oshintil retaliated with a tart remark about sailors and their own primitive propensities, Thonir could tell—with a brief flash of jealousy—that she was pleased his friend had noticed.

In any event, Rishchik confirmed that Thonir had cleared the *Inskirekh-hasot* through customs, and Oshintil paid the boy his fee. Thonir had already said goodbye to Dhokh and a few other crewmen when he and Rishchik left the ship, but now it was time for him to part with Rishchik, as well, something he was loath to do. Although he could certainly hope the first mate would return, he was now sufficiently familiar with the dangers of seafaring to fear that he very well might not.

"Have a safe voyage," he said, as they left the merchant house. "I shall miss you," he added sadly. Sometimes a simple, direct statement of fact is best.

Rishchik grinned. "You stay safe yourself, kid! Our customs authorities are fanatical, and if they ever figure out what you're doing, they'll squash you like a bug."

"Seems like I've had to say a lot of goodbyes these last few months," Thonir told Quirinak moodily when he returned to Madam Shabiril's. "One way or another." He sighed, remembering all the people whom he had come to care about but who were no longer part of his life. "I don't like it. I don't like it one little bit."

"Abandon ship!" suggested Quirinak.

21

The late medieval period saw a surge in pilgrimage activity among those classes that could afford it, chiefly townspeople. The Cantiferians were particularly eager to demonstrate their religious zeal.

— Everyday Life in the Middle Ages

Glip summoned Thonir to interfere with an inspection about once a week thereafter, on average, giving the boy ample time to pursue his own interests. The humble clothes he had received from Gorta the tanner's wife fit him better following a growth spurt over the summer, but he could now afford to commission much nicer ones from an upscale tailor. He also began to shave, taking a few pointers from Madam Shabiril, who had been very particular concerning her late husband's grooming. Finally, to the extent that his hair had grown since being cut aboard the *Porpoise,* Thonir gathered it into the beginnings of a ponytail. Oshintil teased him over his efforts to become a young man of fashion, but he did not mind in the least, responding with an uncharacteristic grin.

Thonir's ample remuneration also permitted him to buy parchments, and he spent hours using Chodros's self-inking quill to record every spell he could remember. It was a precise and laborious job, but he knew that forgetting spells he rarely used was a genuine danger, and he was determined to retain such knowledge as he had at his disposal.

Despite these and other expenditures, Thonir's hoard of silver grew, prompting him to buy a small lockbox, which he protected with security spells. As time drew on, he also exchanged twenty *poog* for a gold *troog,* which he could conceal in his belt.

✦

Money alone, however, was insufficient to quell a vague feeling of dissatisfaction that slowly built as the weeks passed in Shindesh. Thonir had been born on the twenty-fourth day of the Ondiric month of Taaltar. The Esdir employed a different calendar, but Taaltar began with the autumnal equinox, enabling the boy to simply count the days thereafter until he turned seventeen. When the time arrived, Madam Shabiril made him an excellent supper, with extra fruit for Quirinak, but Thonir could not help taking the opportunity to look back and wonder if he had gone astray. In the months since Chodros's arrest, he had done some things he was not proud of—though he was more ashamed of certain things he had failed to do. Either way, there was no getting around certain facts: his training as a wizard had ceased, he was engaged in an illegal enterprise, and he was infatuated with a woman he dared not court. On balance, he did not feel very celebratory.

Thonir's dissatisfaction came to a head three weeks later, while thwarting the inspection of a departing cog called the *Desgrenokh,* or "Storm Petrel," which had taken on an Ondiric sorceress as a passenger. Though no older than twenty, she had not only completed her training in sorcery but learned a surprising amount of wizardry, as well.

Indeed, in exchange for his teaching her the befuddling spell, she was able to teach *him* a wizarding spell to prevent food from spoiling in warm weather. Quite pretty herself, she was traveling in the company of an absurdly handsome knight, who—far from treating her as a helpless female—clearly respected her and deferred to her authority. When Thonir compared this remarkable young woman's accomplishments with what he saw as his own failures, he could not help but ask himself whether the time had come for him to take action: to leave Shindesh, follow Ghenrish's advice, and seek a new master in the Esdiric capital.

By the time he returned to the merchant house with the ship's captain to receive his pay, he had made his decision. He would go.

"I'm leaving," he told Oshintil. "I'm going to Feldross to resume my training in wizardry."

The treasurer raised her elegant eyebrows. "Well, good for you!" she said warmly. "I'll miss having such a faithful admirer, of course, but I'm happy for you." She gave him a beguiling smile. "The *Moshinggok* is sailing first thing tomorrow morning, though. Could I possibly persuade you to work your magic one more time before you leave?"

Thonir blushed fiercely, both because he thought he had kept his admiration secret and because that smile could persuade him to do almost anything.

As it happened, Thonir was already familiar with the *Moshinggok,* or "Monkfish." On the ship's arrival three days earlier, he had persuaded customs that it carried a cargo of nearly worthless sheep bones. In the morning he therefore went directly to the docks without stopping at the merchant house. As he approached, however, he saw that something had gone wrong. Multiple customs inspectors in their yellow jerkins were already aboard—two of them being engaged in a clamorous argument with the captain—while a full squad of twelve royal soldiers in leather armor stood guard on the pier, brandishing an intimidating array of polearms. Evidently, the Royal Esdiric Customs Inspectorate had grown skeptical that the House of Ghilgesh had really switched over to trading exclusively in duty-free rubbish. Thonir had warned the merchants that this might happen, but just like Dob, they had let greed override elementary prudence. He hastily diverted his steps to a different ship, and from there away. At least the customs men did not seem to know precisely how the scam worked, he told himself, or they would have tried to catch him in the act.

Nevertheless, he knew they would be onto him soon. He would have to flee—but first he must warn Oshintil. As he neared the merchant house, however, he saw that he was too late: royal soldiers had surrounded the building, and customs men were leading away various members of the merchant family. To Thonir's dismay, Oshintil was among them, her head held defiantly high. They had not bound her hands, as they had the men's, but Thonir shuddered, having little doubt that she would soon be subjected to shameful mistreatment. King Choofren's men were not known for their humane handling of prisoners. As he watched, additional customs men emerged from the building with stacks of documents, including Oshintil's incriminating ledgers, which they loaded onto a handcart.

Hoping for an opportunity to free Oshintil, he followed at a discreet distance, as the customs men escorted their prisoners back to the Inspectorate. When no such opportunity presented itself, Thonir realized he would have to create one. He therefore caused the contents of the handcart to ignite, using a special magic fire that would be hard to extinguish. The spell was gratifyingly effective as a diversion, as well as a means of destroying evidence, but one of the customs men guarding Oshintil refused to be distracted and seized her roughly by the arm to prevent her from escaping. The man desisted a moment later, however, when his hair burst into flames. Then, notwithstanding the commotion, a nearby soldier suddenly fell asleep, swaying on his feet for a moment, before he lost hold of his poleaxe and collapsed onto the street. Oshintil saw her chance and ran. One of the customs men tried to pursue her but collided with an invisible barrier that knocked him down—rather painfully by the look of it—enabling Oshintil to disappear down a side street.

Unable to follow her without calling attention to himself, Thonir slipped away in another direction. Knowing that his rather flamboyant display of magic would only increase the urgency with which the authorities would try to identify the merchant house's magician, he hastened back to his lodgings to gather his things for departure. Although he saw no one out front, he sneaked in by the back door, remaining alert to the possibility of ambush even as he climbed the stairs to his room.

He found Glip waiting for him, along with Madam Shabiril, who was playing with Quirinak.

"There's shit goin' down out there," warned Glip. "Stay away from the merchant house!"

"Shit goin' down!" repeated Quirinak brightly.

"I know," said Thonir. "I've just come from there." He looked around the room. "I need to pack my things and go. Madam Shabiril, do you have an old sack I can use?"

His landlady nodded. "Of course, dear." She headed for the stairs.

Thonir began to gather up his belongings, placing them on the bed. "The House of Ghilgesh won't survive this," he told Glip, "which means, I think, that you have your freedom, if you're prepared to take it." He dispelled the trap that prevented anyone from removing his lockbox from its place on his small bedside table. "You can come with me, if you like, or you can stay here with Madam Shabiril. The rent's paid through the end of the week, and I'll cover another fortnight, if you like. It's up to you."

Glip grinned. "I'll stay here, thanks. The old gal's nice enough, and I don't think the customs men'll be too interested in me. Plus, there's folk around who'll hire a good errand boy."

Thonir fed Quirinak a nut from a small bag he had enchanted to keep the greedy bird from pilfering. "Sounds like a plan. But you be careful! And if they come looking for me, be helpful. Tell them I was headed for Feldross. Oh, and you can say my real name is Sogpar. I was only calling myself Thonir to conceal my dark criminal past."

"Sogpar," repeated Glip, grinning even wider. "Got it."

Some fifteen minutes later, Thonir crept out the back door with Quirinak perched on his shoulder and his belongings bundled in a large flour sack. More goodbyes, he reflected sadly. More life stories he would never watch unfold. He regretted not being headed for Feldross, but he had no way of knowing whom Oshintil might have told of his earlier intention. Moreover, the authorities might recapture the lovely treasurer herself. No, it was safer to defer his ambitions for the time being and flee elsewhere.

He made his way cautiously to the city's so-called "Pigeon Gate," on the western side of town, with the intention of attaching himself to some group of travelers on the coastal road. Thonir had no firm grasp of Esdiric geography, but he had grown up in a port city, so he would feel safer following the coast than pushing into the unknown interior.

Just inside the gate he found twenty-nine Cantiferian pilgrims, readily identifiable as such by the holy symbols several of them held aloft. Most of the party had horses or donkeys of various types and qualities, but a few were afoot. Spring might be the traditional time to go on pilgrimage, but Thonir knew that Cantiferians had a particular fondness for these undertakings, and the mild autumn weather of the south was a fine inducement for setting out on one. In any event, joining a party of pilgrims would suit Thonir's purposes perfectly. He therefore approached a group of four men without mounts.

"Where are you headed, my brothers?" he asked.

"The shrine of our Holy Sister Shkrig," replied a young, thin, birdlike man. "In Khoriff," he added helpfully, having noticed Thonir's foreign accent.

"In Khoriff!" repeated Quirinak, with an eager head-bob.

"By the saints and profits!" exclaimed Thonir, though he had never heard of Shkrig and had no idea where Khoriff might be. "What a lucky co-, um, coince-, er—"

"Coincidence?" suggested the birdlike man.

"Yes, thank you, brother. Coincidence. For I am headed there myself. May I perhaps join you?"

"Verily, I should think so, brother," said a middle-aged man with a flourishing mustache, "but you'll have to ask our guide." He pointed to a plump man in a green tabard, astride a fine chestnut palfrey. "He arranged this little excursion of ours."

Thonir approached the man, whose puffy cheeks somewhat resembled those of a golden hamster. Having never seen one of those creatures, Thonir just thought him a trifle odd-looking. "Good day, brother," he said. "I understand you organized this pilgrimage to Khoriff. I, too, am headed there, to worship at the shrine of our holy sister. May I travel along with you?"

The pilgrims' guide looked down from his horse. "There is a small fee," he said, smiling, "in recognition of my humble efforts in making the arrangements." He took in Thonir's fashionable clothes. "You have no horse?"

Thonir shook his head. "I have left her at home. I prefer to walk to holy sites."

The guide looked slightly mystified. He was not himself a religious man. "One *poog,*" he said. "Payable in advance."

"Dragon's breath!" said Quirinak.

Thonir considered the sum to be exorbitant but made no demur, instead handing over the requested silver. "When do we leave?" he asked.

The guide briefly examined the coin, then pocketed it. "Now," he replied.

22

The harsh reign of King Choofren III resulted in two separate mass uprisings among the Esdiric peasantry, with many attendant atrocities against the upper classes. Both revolts were ultimately suppressed with surpassing cruelty.

— A Concise but Complete History of World Events

The road to Khoriff did not follow the coast, but proceeded broadly westward through gently rolling terrain, where the downtrodden Esdiric peasantry was finishing up the harvest. Thonir walked at the back of the party with the four men he had first met, to whom he now introduced himself as Fenith, the devout scion of a Cantiferian merchant family from distant Vildenon. The thin, birdlike man revealed himself to be a journeyman carpenter, while the fellow with the luxuriant mustache proved to be a weaver. The other two were a cook and a potter. To pass the time they told ribald tales in verse, for fabliaux about naughty young women and foolish older men were popular in Esdiron at the time. As a result, both Thonir and Quirinak learned some interesting new words. When it was his turn, Thonir told the Ondiric folktale of Favitol the Savage Rooster, translating it as best he could into Esdiric, though he had trouble with some of the vocabulary, notably the words "vainglorious" and "flibbertigibbet," but also a few anatomical terms specific to domestic fowl, such as "comb," "wattles," and "hackles."

172

While his listeners might have preferred a spicier tale, the story was rather humorous, and it did succeed in making them laugh.

In the evenings, Thonir got acquainted with some of the other pilgrims, who came from a variety of social strata—from a knight and his squire to an unskilled laborer who had been saving his coppers for this holy purpose over the course of twelve years. The squire, who was nineteen, took a supercilious attitude toward Thonir, who purported to be merely merchant-class, after all, and was a foreigner to boot. Luckily, not everyone was so standoffish. Several pilgrims showed an interest in Quirinak, for few had ever seen a parrot before, and the sociable bird was always happy to be the center of attention.

The first signs of trouble came when the pilgrims were nearly halfway to Khoriff. At mid-morning they saw distant smoke off to their right, as though some large building were ablaze. An hour or so later, they spotted more smoke, this time beyond a large stand of trees to their left. Thonir noticed that the peasants were missing from the fields, but as a city boy he was unsure what significance to assign to their absence. Around noon, the party arrived in a village, where the guide had arranged for them to take lunch, but the streets were deserted and the tavern was shuttered. No one answered their knock. The village had a Tiralist temple, however, and as they passed, the priest came out. He was an old man wearing a distinctive multicolored vestment with a tasseled cap.

"The peasantry has risen," he warned. "Risen against the fine lords and ladies who live so high off their humble labor. Risen against the tax farmers who so cruelly oppress them. Risen against anyone who does not earn his bread by the sweat of his brow."

There was consternation among the pilgrims. Their guide pressed for details.

"The peasants are enraged by harsh new exactions in connection with the harvest," the priest explained. "By all reports the revolt is sweeping the countryside far and wide. Here in our vicinity, Baron Squench was butchered most barbarously in his own castle yesterday, together with his wife, children, and many of his noble household, some of whom were hunted down like rats and slain on the road, as they sought to escape. Erishog the tax collector, likewise, was torn to pieces and his flesh fed to the dogs." He shook his head despondently. "'Tis a terrible reckoning that has come!"

A great hubbub broke out. The guide declared his intent to return to the safety of Shindesh, and most of the pilgrims, especially the well-born, clamored to accompany him. A few of the more lowly, however, opted to continue on to Khoriff.

"I ain't no nobleman," declared the unskilled laborer who had saved so long for the journey, "nor yet a taxman. These rebels, they got no quarrel with me, nor me with them."

"You're a fool," exclaimed the knight. "These peasants are animals!"

A well-dressed man of about sixty with a spirited white horse unexpectedly announced that he would travel on to Khoriff, as well. "I will come to no harm," he assured the guide, who expressed incredulity at his decision. He was tall with thinning hair and a rather unfortunately proportioned nose. "And I know the way. Someone should."

"Way?" queried Quirinak. "Weigh anchor!"

Thonir tried to consider his options rationally. He knew there was no safety for him in Shindesh, while he could hope that changing out of his fashionable new clothes and back into the ones Gorta had given him would enable him to blend in better with the pilgrims who meant to continue the journey. In addition to the unskilled laborer and the well-dressed horseman, these included the carpenter, the cook, and the potter, but not the weaver. Sticking with the larger party, by contrast, would ally Thonir with a group of people more likely to incur the rebels' wrath. He took his hair out of its ponytail. "I'm sorry," he told the guide, "but I'm going on to Khoriff. I hope all of you make it back safely to Shindesh."

Everyone in the much diminished party of six men, one horse, and an emerald-green parrot was on edge as they resumed their westward march. Going without lunch did not help. Thonir established that the well-dressed man's name was Vishkogak, but no one was in the mood for conversation, so he learned nothing further. They saw more smoke in the distance and sometimes smelled it on the wind. After two hours they came to another village, where three badly mutilated bodies were hanging from the branches of a lone oak on the village square. Thonir felt a visceral fear at the gruesome sight, but it was a fear coupled with anger.

However valid the rebels' grievances, no one deserved such treatment.

"These bodies are fresh," Vishkogak observed. "We should not linger."

Just then the door of the village tavern opened and several peasants emerged. "Looks like we got us another fine gentleman here, boys!" one of them shouted, pointing at Vishkogak. More peasants spilled out onto the square, some clearly the worse for drink.

"String 'im up!" shouted another.

"S-saints and prophets preserve us!" exclaimed the cook, his voice quavering. The carpenter and the manual laborer unsheathed the knives they carried on their belts. Thonir broke into a cold sweat.

"Go," the carpenter told Vishkogak. "They'll never catch a man on horseback. Don't worry. We'll be all right."

Vishkogak shook his head. "I am not leaving you to them."

"Are you crazy?" screamed the potter. "You'll get us all killed. Lookit them weapons!"

Indeed, as they fanned out to surround the pilgrims, many of the roughly two dozen peasants were brandishing various dangerous implements, including hatchets, knives, and the perhaps requisite pitchforks.

Vishkogak sat up taller in the saddle. "We are but humble pilgrims," he declared, "headed for the shrine of the blessed Saint Shkrig in the holy city of Khoriff. I entreat you to let us go in peace."

"Screw some scabby whore of a saint," retorted one of the peasants. "What's she ever done for us?" There was some mild dissent among the crowd, now that the matter had been framed as a religious question, but for the most part the peasants remained intent on violence.

Notwithstanding the fear gripping his insides, Thonir quietly cast his befuddling spell, first on one, then on another of the peasants who had spoken, for he knew that a mob is ruled by its angriest voices.

"We haven't done you any harm," the carpenter pointed out. "And killing us won't reduce your taxes or forgive your debts or cancel your labor obligations."

"Mebbe not," shouted one of the younger peasants, "but watchin' you city folk dance at the end of a rope—that'll still be fun!"

Ignoring some shouts of agreement from among the rougher elements, one of the older peasants rapped the younger one on the side of the head. "That's enough, Firgakh." He turned to the carpenter. "Most of youse look to be ordinary workin' men. We got no quarrel with honest labor. Give us this fancy fellow and his very fine horse, and the rest o' youse can be on yer way." He gestured with open hands as though presenting an eminently reasonable business proposition. "Fair enough?"

Thonir swallowed hard. Any such deal would be shameful, but it *was* a way out. He had befuddled only two more peasants by now, not nearly enough to prevent the mob from working its will. He could try charming someone, but a single peasant arguing for mercy seemed unlikely to carry the day. Thonir's eye strayed to the three bodies dangling from the oak, and his anger stirred again. Whatever the risk, he would not stand by as these murderous yokels claimed another victim, this time for nothing more than the crime of being well-dressed. He had to do something, even if it was just a bluff.

"No," he declared, as firmly as he could. "We won't be doing that." He took a deep breath, ignoring a squeal of dismay from the potter. "Know that I am a fully trained wizard. This demonic green bird is my familiar spirit." ("Demonic green familiar spirit!" repeated Quirinak helpfully.) "And by the seven devils of Gorsach, I swear I'll summon the fires of hell itself to burn alive anyone who tries to harm this man."

There was a brief silence, as the crowd digested this challenging assertion.

"What a load of horseshit!" shouted a peasant who had not spoken before. "Whoever heard of a wizard dressed like an ostler's boy?"

Vishkogak gave a wry laugh. "The man's got a point," he observed mordantly. "Usually they dress a lot more like *me!*" Then, making a broad circular gesture above his head, he gave a great cry in the wizarding tongue, and a ring of magical fire sprang up around the pilgrims. Four peasants, who had unwisely chosen this moment to advance, found themselves in the midst of the crackling flames and leaped back, screaming, their clothes alight, while the others backed hastily away, or fled the scene entirely, as the diameter of the blaze rapidly expanded to encompass most of the village square.

Inside the ring, the pilgrims' sudden proximity to towering flames and searing heat was disconcerting to say the least. Quirinak squawked in alarm, while Vishkogak's high-strung horse reared, throwing the wizard from the saddle.

Fortunately, the carpenter and the unskilled laborer had the presence of mind to grab the reins and managed to bring the skittish animal under control. The potter, by contrast, dropped into a defensive crouch, and the cook fell over him while backing away from the flames.

For a moment, Thonir scarcely understood what was happening. He had been about to set fire to the clothes of the peasant who had scoffed at his claim to mystical powers, when Vishkogak's spell intervened—along with a great deal of confusing noise. Looking around, he was at a loss to see anything useful he could do.

The ring of fire showed no signs of burning out. It thus continued to shield the pilgrims, giving them time to calm down and cope with the situation. Vishkogak had shattered his left wrist in the fall from his horse, but no one else was hurt. After throwing his anesthetizing spell to alleviate the wizard's pain, Thonir helped the carpenter immobilize the broken bones, using a traveling spell book they found in Vishkogak's saddlebags as a makeshift splint and spare clothes from the same source as bandages to bind them together. The two then used more clothes to fashion an improvised sling.

"The seven devils of Gorsach!" chuckled Vishkogak, as the carpenter and Thonir finished up and helped him remount his horse. "I had an inkling you might have magical training, young man."

"How was that?" asked Thonir, surprised.

"I heard your parrot repeat a wizarding incantation last night," he replied. "The bird had to pick it up from someone!" When the pilgrims were ready to leave, Vishkogak dispelled the ring of fire, which vanished as abruptly as it had appeared, leaving dramatic scorch marks on the village square, along with an unpleasant smell. A few peasant rebels still lurked in the vicinity, but they gave the departing pilgrims a wide berth. Once clear of the village, Vishkogak turned to Thonir. "I would be interested to hear your story."

23

Feldross is a bustling modern city, due in large part to its thorough-going redesign in the middle years of the last century —a pioneering urban-planning project that created the broad, tree-lined avenues that are now filled with motor traffic. . . . Travelers are well advised, however, to master at least a few key Esdiric phrases, for the otherwise cosmopolitan inhabitants of Feldross are notorious for snubbing Ondirophone visitors.

— *The Motor-Tourist's Guide to Esdiron* (1st ed.)

Thonir felt he needed to trust Vishkogak with the truth, but since he was reluctant to share the incriminating details with the other pilgrims, he cast a spell to muffle their conversation, as the party continued its march westward. He then confessed his misadventures since Chodros's arrest.

Vishkogak gave his story careful attention. "I don't see that you behaved so very badly under the circumstances," he said, when Thonir finished. "Not that the Esdiric customs authorities would agree. Or the Mindoric criminal courts, for that matter. I take it you still wish to resume your magical training?"

Thonir assured him that he did.

Vishkogak gave him a searching look. "Very well, I will take you on," he said. "There's room enough for you in my house in Feldross. Besides, it will be helpful to have a resourceful apprentice while my wrist is healing."

181

Although the rest of the journey to Khoriff remained fraught with danger, as the peasant uprising roiled the countryside, the two wizards worked together to frighten off the rebels they met, so that in the end the pilgrims arrived at their destination safely and without actually killing anyone. The other pilgrims shook their heads in amazement at the demonstrations of wizardry, and thanked the blessed Saint Shkrig for what they took to be her benevolence in thus assuring their safe passage to her shrine.

Upon arrival in Khoriff, Vishkogak went directly to a healer, who set his broken bones and put his wrist in a cast. This might have been a painful business, but Thonir again applied his anesthetizing spell to good effect. The pilgrims had to stay in Khoriff longer than they planned, however, as the revolt ran its blood-drenched course, followed by its even more terrible suppression. In the meantime, they venerated Shkrig, purchased inexpensive souvenirs, and waited. Thonir had an awkward moment, when he admitted to Vishkogak that he had not been raised in the Cantiferian faith and actually had no firm religious views, but the older wizard accepted these admissions without rebuke.

As the days shortened, the weather turned colder. While safe, the return journey was harrowing all the same, given the party's frequent encounters with the decomposing remains of rebellious peasants, displayed like vermin on a gamekeeper's gibbet. Although the travelers were spared the sight of the climactic battlefield, some twenty leagues to the north, where armored knights had slaughtered the rebel army, the evidence of violent death they did see was enough. Even the usually irrepressible Quirinak took his cue from the rest of the party and grew reticent.

Admittedly, Thonir's spirits lifted upon reaching Feldross. Although prudence dictated that he continue to go by Fenith—or rather "Fenit," as the Esdir pronounced it—he felt newly secure under Vishkogak's aegis. Above all, he was an apprentice again, relearning the spells he had lost, but also venturing into new and more complex magicks, while living in a big and exciting city. He missed some of the friends he had made that year, but Vishkogak proved a knowledgeable and good-natured master, Quirinak made an entertaining companion, and the alchemist whose shop they frequented employed an intriguing female assistant of about Thonir's own age, with whom he was determined to get better acquainted.

Soon it was time for the feast of the winter solstice, a significant event in the Cantiferian calendar. Vishkogak invited two other local wizards to partake of the household's festive meal, which consisted of no fewer than eight courses and three different wines. Although his wrist was still in its cast, he had devised a clever spell to chop his food into bite-sized pieces without the use of his hands. Thonir was pleased. Not only had he learned something about inventing new spells in the process, he no longer had to chop up Vishkogak's food himself.

"That cook of yours has outdone herself tonight, Vishko," the younger of the two visiting wizards remarked, as they finished generous servings of roast duck with lentils and mushrooms. He was a strange-looking man with many scars on his face, neck, and hands.

Judging from the first five courses, at least, Thonir thought the meal was likely the best he had ever eaten, and said so.

Although the older guest, who was well into his eighties, believed that apprentices (or anyone under the age of about thirty-five, for that matter) should be seen and not heard, he did no more than gaze disapprovingly at Thonir for a moment, before remarking on the shocking recent increase in the price of parchment.

Vishkogak acknowledged that the cook deserved praise. He also noted that the treasury's insistence on debasing the *poog* was resulting in higher prices across the board. "Speaking of parchment, though," he added, "it's remarkable how much having a diligent apprentice increases one's outlay for basic materials. Fenit, I noticed this morning that our stock of fresh parchment is running low, so I'll have to take you out to the tanner's tomorrow and introduce you. I'm afraid you'll have work enough there to keep you busy for awhile."

Well aware of the dire state of the supply cupboard, Thonir ate the last mushroom on his plate, looked at his master, and smiled. "It will be my pleasure, Eminence."

And he did not even mean it ironically.

About the Author

Sedigitus Swift is a historian by day and a pseudonymous fantasy author by night (as well as during eclipses or otherwise under cover of darkness). When not diverting himself by writing offbeat medieval fantasy novellas, he specializes in the perplexities of modern Central and Eastern Europe. No doubt he has other equally perverse interests, but we are not currently certain exactly what those might be.

If you have enjoyed this book, why not subscribe to his engaging monthly newsletter, *The News from Ondiran,* at www.sedigitus.com, for advance word on upcoming works, insights into the creative process, and choice bits of Ondiric lore? It's free!

And if you're feeling really benevolent, you might leave favorable online reviews anywhere such reviews congregate. They don't have to be long or detailed, but they will help other readers find this book.

Be on the lookout or *The Court Sorcerers,* Book Five in this series, coming soon!

www.sedigitus.com

Also from *Archelaus*

The Corpse in the Trash Room
by Colette Tajemna

In a college dorm in the late Seventies, seven hallmates hold a funeral for a pet hamster, only to stumble upon a body . . .

Startled but not exactly sorrowful at finding their unpopular dorm preceptor slumped atop a garbage can in the trash room, Keith and his friends can't resist investigating, and set to questioning a quirky set of potential witnesses and suspects. Could the killer be a fellow student? A member of the faculty or staff? The provost? Might it even be one of their friends?

Keith and his pals must navigate college politics, unruly druggies, and lesbian separatists in order to uncover the truth!